Seven Openings of the Head

© Liane Keightley, 2007

Edited by Andy Brown
Cover photographs by Andrew Dent

Library and Archives Canada Cataloguing in Publication

Keightley, Liane
Seven openings of the head / Liane Keightley.

ISBN 978-1-894994-24-8

I. Title.
PS8571.E44578S49 2007   C813'.54   C2007-905948-1

Dépot legal, Bibliothèque nationale du Québec
Printed and bound in Canada on 100% recycled,
ancient rainforest-friendly paper.
First Edition

conundrum press
PO Box 55003, CSP Fairmount,
Montreal, Quebec, H2T 3E2, Canada
conpress@ican.net
www.conundrumpress.com

Acknowledgements
Many, many thanks to Taien Ng-Chan, Dana Bath,
Francesca LoDico, Meg Sircom, Andrew Dent, Joshua
Karpati, Rob Allen, and the Canada Council for the
Arts. An extra special thanks to Andy Brown. And to
Harper Levine, for telling me to write in the first place.

conundrum press acknowledges the financial assistance of the
Canada Council for the Arts toward our publishing program.

Canada Council   Conseil des Arts
for the Arts   du Canada

Seven Openings of the Head

Stories by

Liane Keightley

CONTENTS

No One Tells You 7

You Were Always the Kind One 29

The Channel Swimmer 41

Inlet 57

Ten-Cent Packs 69

Seven Openings of the Head 85

Triton and Tex 101

NO ONE TELLS YOU

"You are a bad man," Kit said with gentle clarity. "You don't care about anyone but yourself." The car was struggling up a long, drawn-out hill, so she shifted into fourth. "If you had a child you would neglect it. If your father fell ill, you'd put him in a home and never visit." Levy was staring out the passenger window while Kit spoke, looking, it seemed, at something far beyond the landscape. "You feel no remorse, and you never apologize for your bad behaviour." She was trying to get at something, feeling her way towards it without being quite sure what it was. "I've never seen you cry," she tried. "Or put another person's needs first." And here it was, she'd found it. "I think it's possible that you aren't even human."

She looked over at him, trying to gauge his response. She needed something from him here, she needed to shake something loose. But he hadn't shifted his gaze. "What do you think?" she asked, as if she'd been trying out an acceptance speech on him. She looked back and forth between him and the highway unfolding in front of them.

Still looking out the passenger window, Levy smiled a great big crooked-toothed smile, a smile that made her think he was about to guffaw, as if she'd said something unexpectedly funny. "You may be right," he said, still looking out at the trees passing them by. After a moment, though, he stopped smiling. He turned and looked at her for the first time since they'd begun arguing. His hair was greasy. A thick strand of it stuck to his right temple, and she saw that he had a chewed down pencil tucked behind his ear like a nineteenth-century merchant. She pictured him in an oilcloth apron, then imagined him in glasses. She thought glasses might suit him. When he was older and needed them to read, she would enjoy reaching out to him in bed and gently slipping them off him. Then the thought turned sour.

"I'm sorry," he said, "that you feel so lonely with me."

They were coming down the other side of the hill. Kit looked in the rearview mirror at the line of cars stretched out for half a mile behind them on the highway. They floated down the hill like the long, disjointed tail of a Chinese dragon. "What are you talking about," she said, and practically snorted. She gripped the steering wheel with both hands and looked back to the road ahead.

Levy turned again to the trees. He was wearing his favourite sweater. It had two small moth holes at the shoulder. The beginning of the end. But he looked good in it. "You know what I'm talking about," he said to the trees.

During the long period of silence that followed, they left the highway and began to navigate the uncertain terrain of forest and back roads. Wind whistled through the air vent. The car thumped and shuddered across the pocked asphalt.

For no good reason, Levy said, "You should have made a left back there." Looking out at the trees he'd started feeling a pioneering masculinity, that had suddenly bloomed into a previously non-existent instinct for where he was headed.

"Do you think?" Kit said, looking back over her shoulder. "Where's the map?"

Kit had a faith in maps that annoyed Levy. Maps made him nervous in a vague, sea-sick sort of way. When he unfolded a map in a car and spread it awkwardly across his lap, he experienced a feeling of helplessness that irritated him. The final logic of them eluded him. But he had to stand his ground, so he pulled the map out from where it had slid between the seats. He swept his finger across it until he found a hopeful-looking spot, a spot that might well have been them. "Yeah, that was it," he said. He felt in the grip of something he couldn't name and was unable to resist. He felt giddy. He watched her as she scanned the road for signs. She believed him. She trusted him. He liked the way she looked when she was driving. Her face was serious, no-nonsense.

"Shit," she said.

It was early in the day and her face was still a little puffy. In the mornings her face was always that way. There was an element of the grotesque about it that fascinated him. It made her look vulnerable. He could see now, in the natural light, the lines that had begun to settle in permanently. He could see what she was going to look like when she was an older woman. He thought she would be striking, instead of merely pretty. A sadness had leaked into her demeanor lately and he wondered if this was contributing to the impression.

"Turn up here," he said, "this'll take us back." He pointed ahead at a patch of grass.

"That's not a road," she said, slowing down.

He tapped the map like a school teacher. "Yes it is."

It looked simply like an opening in the trees. "I don't think so," she said.

He tapped harder, impatiently. "It's on the map." The map was now his irrefutable ally.

She had come to a stop now, and was staring down the grassy path that was mysteriously on the map. This was not a way back. He knew this was what she was thinking. But she took the turn, to make amends. He knew her that well. He put his hand on her thigh and gave it a squeeze, then felt a rush of desire for her. He squeezed her thigh again, then slid his hand under the hem of her skirt to her bare flesh.

"No," she said, shoving his hand away without even turning to look at him. He retreated to his side of the car and went back to looking out at the trees.

He didn't want children. It was a tragedy she hadn't seen coming. "We'll get a dog," he'd said, to soften the pronouncement. It had been a Saturday night, and he was lying on the couch watching the game with the sound off. Turning off the sound was his concession to the conversation she'd started. It turned out that he had been indulging her talk of a child, playing along as if it were merely another kind of sex talk.

Two months before that Saturday conversation she'd gone off the pill, and he had turned to condoms like a drunk to an AA meeting. She'd thought he simply wasn't ready yet. She didn't understand how two people who spent so much time together could want such different things.

Since that evening she hadn't been sleeping well. She felt on edge most days, with a vague sense that she was waiting for something. She'd hoped for a clear feeling of resolve, like she'd experienced after that Saturday night conversation. Anger had been her ally. But instead, in the weeks that followed, she'd let things simply continue, returning to the way they'd been before the conversation. They did the things they'd always done. But she felt as if these things had become covered in a grey film, as if she'd thrown the black wash in with the whites.

"This is it," Levy said. They'd been driving along a rough gravel road for fifteen minutes with nothing in sight.

"But there's no sign," Kit said. She slowed down and turned into the driveway but didn't turn off the engine.

"It's the only place around." He waved a crumpled piece of paper in the air between them. "The agent's directions were very clear."

She looked at him sitting there hesitating, trying his best to size up the house. "Levy," she said. When he turned towards her she took his hand and kissed it. He held onto hers and bit it softly.

"You look very pretty today," he said.

"You too." She held his hand firmly in hers. It had the amplified warmth of an egg plucked from a nest. Sometimes he is like a child that needs protecting, she thought. I can do that for him. I can protect him. Then she caught herself and quietly extricated her hand.

This was all for Levy's brother, who'd broken his leg in a car accident two days before. "If you could just check to see if it's a dump or not," he'd said. "But don't tell them you're not me."

"Why?" Levy had asked, looking at him suspiciously.

"Just don't. I think the agent likes me. She might be able to get me a deal."

It was unclear why he wanted to buy a place out in the middle of nowhere. He'd gotten divorced eight months before, and since then a return-to-the-land mentality had taken hold of him. But, as Levy liked to point out, he complained about having to shovel the front walk, so it was hard to square the circle.

"It'll be a nice drive anyway," Kit had said.

Levy got out of the car and slammed the door. The exterior of the house depressed him. It looked to him like the scene of a future crime. Something bloody and preventable. They walked up to the house at first holding hands, and then not. The door was standing half-open with a big set of keys dangling from the lock. A fat manila envelope was sticking out from the slot in the open door like an angry tongue. The house itself, a sprawling bungalow, had seen better days, but someone had worked to freshen it up, painting the shutters and the garage door a slick bright blue, and planting daisies along the walk, the earth freshly turned. They stepped through the open door apprehensively. Once they'd made it to the living room, still without having seen anyone, Levy called out, "Hello?" to no reply.

Kit was walking behind him, and had taken hold of the hem of his sweater. "Quit it," he said in a whisper, as if he were planning to make a grab for something portable and expensive, "You'll stretch it." Kit let go, but a moment later she grabbed hold, through the sweater, of a bit of skin on his back and twisted it hard. "Ow!" Levy arched forward to get away, then turned around and gave her his fiercest look. Kit shrugged as if she were innocent, did a thing with the corners of her mouth that said, It wasn't me. "Stop it," Levy hissed, then turned his attention back to the room they'd entered.

It was an austere room, as if its owners had packed up half of its contents in the first stage of a move. Levy hated this kind of emptiness in a room. No proper couch to spend a Saturday afternoon on, a TV the size of a postage stamp. Bare floors and no sign of life. It looked like a room that no one ever used. His aunt had a room like this, a shabby attempt at a show room. What it was trying to show he'd never understood. Everything said, Step back. The piano could have been the saving grace, but the cover was down over the keys with a bleached white doily set across it, the whole thing giving him the cold shoulder.

Kit was standing at the window looking out. "I like the view," she said. "I bet you can watch deer drift out of those woods in the morning." She turned back to the room and walked over to the piano. She was both shy and bold in strange ways, ways he could never quite guess at. She pulled out the stool and sat at the piano, rolling up the doily and putting it on her lap before she lifted the cover and ran her fingers across the length of the keys. She started to sing quietly to herself, lightly picking out the tune on the piano. It sounded nice. He glanced out the window and saw what she meant about the view.

With Kit at the piano the room started to make more sense. It was always a strange thing when that happened. But it often happened with her.

Kit was having trouble getting the song right. She'd always wanted a piano of her own, so she wouldn't have to be so perpetually out of practice. She would teach a child of her own how to play. They would perform duets together, and make up silly words to the songs. Kit had been thinking lately about having a child alone. At first the thought had made her cry. She'd felt somehow that her hands had been tied. So this is love, she'd thought. It made her shake her head. No one tells you this part. How could she possibly leave Levy behind? But the thought of having a child alone persisted, and she wore it around for a while like a new pair of shoes, until calluses started to form and it stopped hurting quite so much.

Kit swivelled around on the stool toward Levy. "The piano's out of tune," she said in a stage whisper. She stood up and put things back the way she'd found them. "It's nice though." She lay her hand on the varnished wood. "Okay, you've convinced me. I'll take it."

"When I make my first hundred-thousand," Levy said.

They kept on moving through the house, and when they got to the kitchen they saw the realtor standing at the stove crying. She was a woman who looked older than she probably was, with a coppery brown bob fresh from the hairdresser's. She dabbed at her eyes expertly with the back of her wrist.

"Oh hi!" she said above the loud rattle of a fan. "Don't worry, it's just the onions!" A mountain of diced onions sat on a cutting board beside a bowl of green peas. "Do you like mint?" she shouted. She reached over and turned off the fan. A small, square pin on the lapel of her jacket flashed in the sunlight when she moved, as if she were sending out a distress signal to anyone who might be watching through the window. She threw the onions into a pan and they sizzled right away.

"Some people say fresh-baked cookies, but I say, fried onions! Nothing is quite so welcoming, don't you think?" She put her hand on her cheek. "Except to children, I imagine." She said this more quietly, as if it were an afterthought that embarrassed her.

She came around to where they stood, drying her hands on a dish towel as she approached, and said, "Mr. Gordon, Madame Bégin, it is *such* a pleasure," and shook their hands like she meant it. "Please, I'd like you to call me Susan." Kit and Levy looked at one other once she'd gone back to her onions. Who did she think she was talking to? They had no idea what kind of things Levy's brother had made up on the phone, but he was known for a certain paranoia.

Susan shuffled over to the old-fashioned fan sitting on a stool. A terrible rattling came up when she turned it on again. It was both a rattling and a screeching, and it was a sound neither Kit nor Levy had ever heard come out of a fan that didn't plan to set your house on fire. When it finally subsided into a gentler pneumatic wheeze they realized that Susan had been speaking to them during the shrieking. "That's just how I feel about it," she summed up, and brushed her hands together as if that were that.

"Well!" she said and clapped her hands against her ample thighs. "It's so nice to meet you, finally! Shall I give you the tour?"

She started in the basement. The rec room, the bathroom, the furnace room, the laundry room. The whole place felt doomed. Standing over the washing machine and peering in, Levy commented on the size of machine. "Oh," she said, "it'll do big loads of, you know, diapers and so on." She smiled happily.

Levy, still peering into the mouth of the machine, said, "A big load in the diaper then a big load in the machine." Susan giggled uncertainly, then began to laugh. She bent in half and silently shook for a long moment and when she stood up straight again tears were running down her rough cheeks. At first Levy continued staring blindly into the machine, grinning discreetly at his unexpected success. But after a moment he looked up and stared at Susan who was practically peeing herself beside him. Even he knew it wasn't that funny.

The yard, according to Susan, was ideal for a child to run around in. The basement stairs would easily accommodate a baby gate. Every mention made Levy wince. Shh, he wanted to say, She'll hear you. He felt protective of Kit, which was new terrain for him. Usually he thought of her as fully capable of protecting herself, and so never went to the trouble on her behalf. Every mention, he knew, was like a pin being jabbed into her vein, and because he thought it, he felt the unpleasant jab in his own. This was new. This was something new.

It began to seem as if she were taunting Kit. "This is the baby's room," she said of a small room off the hallway. Not the spare room, or the guest room, or the office. She gave Kit a significant look, that, charitably, could have been interpreted as a look of encouragement, that consisted of her nearly non-existent eyebrows shooting up towards her forehead in a mockery of surprise. Levy smiled and nodded, working hard to appear oblivious.

There was nothing in the small rectangle of a room to suggest it had previously housed a baby. Or a child of any age. A wooden chair with the fabric seat re-covered in an ugly grey-gold paisley, a single bed with a chipped plaster cross on the wall above it, a chest of drawers that had seen better days, its oak veneer peeling away at the edges as if it were trying to make an escape from the dreary life it had been forced to live in this linoleum-lined room.

The telephone rang in the hallway. Susan looked confused for a moment. It rang again and she seemed eager to pretend that none of them was hearing the ringing. "And this is the closet," she said, groping blindly at the handle while her eyes looked off in the other direction at nothing at all. At the end of the third ring, though, she suddenly appeared to regain her hearing and said, "Oh, excuse me, I need to get that."

Kit and Levy stood alone in the baby room. "It's like a sixteenth-century dungeon in here," Kit said, licking her lips after she'd spoken. "It's like the solitary cell of a balding, virgin monk," she said, refining it, like the set up to a bad joke.

"Monks are virgins by definition," Levy said, sitting on the bed and bouncing up and down. The springs on the bed seemed to be to his liking because he bounced and bounced until his feet started to leave the floor with each bounce. He grinned at her from up in the air. "You look like a lunatic retard," Kit said, staring him down.

"Fuck you," he said, still grinning and bouncing.

"Fuck you," she said back.

From the hallway Susan chirped, "Be right there!"

"A lunatic monk who doesn't get any," she said.

"At least I'm not a withholding monk, who mopes around his cell all day," he said.

"Yes you are."

They continued to stare each other down until they heard Susan coming and Levy stopped the bouncing and got up off the bed.

In the hallway Susan linked arms with Kit. "So?" she asked, "what do you think?" She leaned forward as she spoke in order to peer as directly as possible into Kit's face. Kit panicked at the speed with which Susan's face was approaching her own, so she turned away and coughed, raising her hand as a shield.

"I..." she began, wondering where the hell Levy was. "It's lovely. But I can't say one way or the other just yet." Susan nodded very seriously while Kit spoke.

"No, I understand," she said. She continued nodding to herself. Then she was suddenly leaning in again. "Would a dog be problematic?"

"A dog?"

"Yes, I was thinking of getting one. Something small. But not one of those yappy ones."

"A dog sounds nice," Kit said, feeling that she no longer had a proper hold on the conversation.

"Oh good!" Susan said. "I'm so happy. Here, let me show you the bathroom," and she let go of Kit's arm and hurried ahead.

She seemed to be trying so hard to impress them that Kit was certain the house must have some secret flaw. The more she laughed at Levy's lame jokes the bigger Kit assumed the problem must be. By the time they came back into the kitchen, Kit was convinced the house must be scheduled for demolition.

They stood in the kitchen, all three of them silent. "And of course this is the kitchen," Susan said after a moment, almost compulsively, as if she'd tried and failed to keep from stating the obvious. There was an edge of nervous exhaustion to her voice.

"Well," she said, looking from one to the other. "Let's eat!"

Levy looked at Kit for direction. "I think..." he began.

"We can't stay," Kit said. "We have to get going."

Susan looked crestfallen. "Oh," she said, and looked at the floor. "May I ask," she began and took hold of her own hand as if to comfort herself. For a moment she looked truly afraid. "May I ask what kind of report you're planning to file?"

Levy and Kit both stared at her. Levy felt a sudden rush of heat through his body and then his hands started to sweat.

"Report?"

"Yes," she said, and forced a smile. "A good one, I hope?"

The smell of onions permeated the air. The room seemed to expand and contract.

"Oh yes," Kit finally said in a too-loud voice used on people who caught her off-guard. "A very good one."

They managed to get themselves lost on the way back. After much backtracking they found themselves at a covered bridge they had already crossed over a half-hour before. They had avoided talking about the morning's events by focusing on the tangle of dirt roads, a web intent on trapping them. Levy struggled to decipher the hieroglyphs that stood in for roads and highways and train tracks. There had never been such a concerted effort between them. They worked hard to avoid talking about it. But at the sight of the bridge Kit pulled the car over.

"This is ridiculous," she said. "You can't read a goddamn map."

She pulled a pack of gum out from somewhere in the back seat, took a couple of pieces and handed him the pack, then got out of the car. There wasn't a soul in sight. No farms, no houses, no cars. They were in the middle of nowhere. It had turned into a beautiful day, and a warm breeze had picked up. Levy got out of the car and followed Kit over to the edge of the river.

When he was within a couple of feet of her she reached out and shoved him hard. She caught him off-guard, and he stumbled forward and fell to the ground. He caught himself with his right hand on a gravelly patch of dirt. For a moment he looked up at her, his face frozen in a look of astonishment. Then he sprang up off the ground and ran at her. Half frightened by the look on his face she started to run. He sped up to catch her, but she could run fast, and in a moment he was sprinting after her across the covered bridge and down the dirt road in the direction from which they'd come.

Levy seemed to find previously untapped reserves of speed and energy in the rage that came to him out of nowhere, like a deep and long-ignored hunger. He thought of nothing but pursuit. Of getting his hands on her. After a time, though, he started to flag, and finally had to stop.

He fell forward, his hands on his knees to support himself, and heaved and panted like a man desperately out of shape.

Kit was running for dear life, that's how it felt. The rush of adrenaline could have kept her going forever. She was ready to move and keep on moving. But when she looked over her shoulder and saw Levy far behind, leaning over in defeat, she gradually slowed down, eventually turning around and slowly making her way back toward him. She felt something give inside her, like a bolt being thrown. By the time she reached him he was standing straight again, but still panting heavily.

She reached out and gave his stomach a rough pat. "You're fat and out of shape, mister," she said.

"You," he croaked, and something inside him turned over like a bird falling from a nest. He caught her by surprise, grabbing her around the shoulder and getting her into a head lock. She struggled and managed to get them both onto the ground, but he still had her firmly in a hold. They stayed like that for a while, each working hard to cancel out the efforts of the other.

When her strength began to fail, he shifted his hold and flipped her fully onto the ground. He lay on top of her and pinned her arms above her head. "Christ you're strong," he said, looking into her face. He lay his cheek against hers, then kissed her ear. She reached up and bit his in return. They took hold of each other as if it were all new to them.

"We don't have any condoms," Kit said. She was practically panting now, feeling a desperate need for Levy, as if the choice were not her own. She longed for him even while he was right there with her. For a moment it felt as if it would burn a hole right through her.

"You run fast," Levy said, his hand moving across the contours of her head.

"I swallowed my gum."

A blue jay called out from a tree nearby. Levy ran his hand roughly over Kit's face, like a man suddenly gone blind. "Serves you right," he said. Her skin was sticky and hot under his hand. She smelled of sweat and shampoo. The jay declared itself again.

"I could listen all day," Kit said.

Levy shifted onto his elbow and looked at her. "I love you," he said. He grabbed her face and kissed her. "Do you hear me?" He shook her head to convey the force of his love. "I..." he said, looking frantically into her face, at her eyes that refused to open when he needed to tell her something this important. He kissed her ear, her neck. He didn't know what to do with it.

"I don't care about the condoms. I don't care," he muttered into her neck.

Kit opened her eyes and looked at the side of

Levy's head. His hair was so greasy she could smell it. She realized that she did; she did care about them.

"No, do you hear me? I don't care," he said, when she tried to shift him away.

If you make a mistake, does it matter when? She lay for a long moment wondering this, Levy perched above her, waiting.

YOU WERE ALWAYS THE KIND ONE

An adult driving with her mother is no adult at all.

"Serena," Serena's mother said when they'd been on the road together for less than five minutes, "something smells funny." She sniffed the air like an inquisitive dog. "I think it's you, dear. You smell funny. What have you been *doing*?"

Serena had taken the morning off work to do her mother Betsy this favour. She was behind the wheel of Betsy's car, driving her to her doctor's appointment. They'd left with plenty of time to spare, just the way Betsy liked it. Her mother was keen on taking her own car, but she didn't like to drive it into the city herself, especially on a rainy day. She seemed happy to be freed of the responsibility.

Serena sighed. "If I said that to you, I'd never hear the end of it."

Betsy was well-dressed, as usual, in heels and an expensive skirt. She dug in her purse for a Kleenex but found a roll of butterscotch Life Savers instead. "But what is that smell? It stinks." She opened the roll, popped one in her mouth, then peeled the paper further back and held the roll out to Serena.

"No, thank you."

"Don't be that way." Betsy brought the roll closer to Serena's face and shook it.

"I really don't want one." Serena leaned away from her mother and her Life Savers.

"Alright. Suit yourself." She dropped the roll back in her purse then started digging for something else.

"Your father's sick as a dog," she said, still rummaging in her purse. "He refuses to look after himself." She pulled out her glasses case and then her wallet, placing them on the seat beside her, then dug some more in her purse.

They were on the highway now, passing alongside the miles and miles of electrical towers that loomed under the overcast sky like comical, giant robots — angry shoulders raised, holding up their cables like resentful matrons wading across a river.

"There's a movie in there somewhere," Serena said.

"Hmm?" Betsy said after a long moment. "What's that, dear?" Her search had become all-consuming.

The highway stretched out in front of them, its sameness the only thing worth noting. Serena opened the window so she wouldn't have to talk to her mother.

"Aha!" Betsy's hand finally emerged from her purse, holding up a tube of lipstick as if it were a winning lottery ticket.

Serena glanced at her mother, then away. The robot towers frowned but said nothing.

They stopped twice in the space of fifteen minutes at Betsy's request: once for an iced tea and once for a pee. Serena resisted her mother's request to stop a third time for a newspaper.

"You get sick reading in the car, what's the point?"

"It would be nice to have it, that's all," Betsy said, and turned her whole body toward the passenger window in a show of indignation. "Don't forget whose car this is, Miss."

Her mother chose to pass on the driving responsibilities so that she could tell her daughter how to drive. "Watch out for that pothole, I just had the axle fixed!" and, "Slow down, why are you in such a tearing rush?" When an 18-wheeler came up beside them to pass, she sucked in audibly and gripped the seat. "Watch out, for God's sake!"

The truck was driving along in its own lane, doing nothing particularly dangerous. "Watch out for what?" Serena said in irritation, and her mother started shouting, "Pull this car over! Pull this car over now!" and actually thumped her fist on the dashboard in her rage.

Serena didn't pull over. She took her foot off the gas and let the truck pass as quickly as possible, and when it was far ahead of them and its loud rumble had faded, Betsy seemed to calm down. In fact, she acted as if nothing had happened.

Now Betsy was staring out the passenger window of the car as if in a trance, and Serena was looking straight ahead. The sky suddenly began to clear, as if a hand had risen from the earth with a giant cloth and was wiping the clouds away.

"Oh, the sun!" Betsy said and came back to life. She got her phone out of her purse and started dialing. She was a big fan of her phone. She called everyone she knew the first week she got it. "How're you feeling," she said into the phone now. She sounded like a bored nurse. "Make yourself a cup of tea." They whizzed past a sign for live worms and fresh eggs. "Stop watching golf and go take a nap. You've never played a day in your life. Why the fascination I'll never know." She examined a button on her blouse while Serena's father spoke on the other end. "Yes, yes, everything's fine. Your daughter drives like a bat out of hell, though... Yes, just like you... Turn off the golf for crying out loud. You're not that deaf, are you?"

When she got off the phone she went back to staring out the window. "Your father's getting old," she said philosophically. He'd recently turned seventy, but there were only three years between them. Serena decided not to point this out.

"Let's stop in on Eleanor," Betsy said coming back to life again. Eleanor was an old friend of Betsy's who ran a tea room in a village not far from the old highway. "Eleanor took you to your first movie," she said in an effort to convince Serena. "You used to stand at the end of the driveway waiting for her whenever you knew she was coming to babysit."

"I remember," Serena said. "She always brought me candy."

"Did she? You never told me that." Her mother seemed briefly annoyed at this revelation.

They left the main highway and headed toward the 112. They drove past cornfields and farmhouses until they hit the little village where Eleanor lived. They turned into the lane at the back of the tea room. "How's she doing, anyway?" Serena asked as they pulled into a parking spot and got out of the car.

"Do you know, I haven't talked to Eleanor in six months," Betsy said and slammed the door. "I just don't know where the time goes."

When they walked around to the front, they saw that a piece of loose-leaf had been taped to the outside of the door and was flapping in the breeze. It said, *Closed due to illness*.

Betsy stared at the sign. "Nobody called me," she said. She cupped her hands around her eyes like a scuba diver and peered in through the window. "Nobody told me a thing." She tugged at the locked door, then turned and stared out at the street. She looked as if someone had played a trick on her. "Why didn't she call?"

There was no answer when Serena rang Eleanor's doorbell, and neither of the neighbours was home.

Betsy was quiet when they got back in the car. Serena wasn't sure what to say to her mother. "Why don't you call her right now?" she tried. "You've got your phone. Give her a call and find out what's going on."

Betsy just shook her head and hugged her purse to her stomach, her elbow propped up on the passenger door and her chin in her hand. "I'd rather not talk, if you don't mind," she said, and continued to stare out at the empty fields.

Within a few minutes, though, she turned on the radio and started humming indiscriminately to the music.

After a while she started digging around in her purse. "I should check on your father," she said. "Knowing him, he's lying on the couch eating cookies from the freezer." She shook her head in irritation and sighed, flipped open her phone and began to dial.

Betsy's doctor's office was in a residential neighbourhood in the city. When they arrived, they turned into the alley at the back. The speed bumps made them move slowly, inching their way along the cracked pavement, past great old elms that leaned over the alley from the yards backing onto it. It was a quiet alley, shady and dappled with puddles from the morning's rain. "Look at that!" Betsy said. Serena put her foot on the brake. Straight ahead, there was a squirrel drinking from one of the puddles, its nose touching the surface of the water and its tail straight up and out behind it, as though it were about to do a cartwheel.

After a moment, Betsy stated the obvious. "He's not moving," she said. The squirrel seemed strangely frozen in place, his body stretched out long from nose to tail. Not a twitch, not a blink.

"What do you think he's doing?" Serena asked her mother. Her mother was the expert. She had always been the one who came running out of the house with a bucket of water to throw at the squirrels who dug in her garden.

"I don't know," Betsy answered.

"That seems like an unnatural position for a squirrel."

"It does."

"What do you think he's thinking in that squirrelly brain of his? 'If I stand perfectly still they'll think I'm a reflection'?"

Betsy thought for a moment. "Maybe he was hit by lightning," her mother said.

Serena looked at her mother to see if she was serious. "During the rain this morning?" she said, trying to follow her mother's train of thought.

"Maybe."

Serena looked at the squirrel. "Well why didn't he fall over?"

"I don't know," Betsy said, "maybe he seized up from the shock of it."

"Creatures don't seize up like that when they die."

Betsy considered this. "Sometimes they do," she finally said.

They were both silent. Serena found herself wanting to believe her mother, even though it didn't make any sense.

"I wonder if we should move him," Betsy said, and seemed to both hope and fear that Serena would pooh-pooh this idea.

"No, no," Serena said, softened by her mother's concern, "stay in the car. We'll go around him." But they could both see that there was no way around. The lane was too narrow.

"Well we have to go or you'll be late for your appointment," Serena said, suddenly tired of the whole thing.

"No! You'll knock his tail right off him! It's so pretty the way it's standing up."

Serena looked at her mother in disbelief. "This is ridiculous," she said, and laid her foot on the gas pedal.

"No!" Betsy shouted, opening the door and leaping out.

Serena hit the brake hard, and the open door bounced back and knocked Betsy over.

From where Betsy sat on the pavement she saw the squirrel reanimate and run off toward the elms.

"Mom! Are you alright?" Serena ran around to where her mother was sitting on the ground and squatted down beside her.

"Mom, are you hurt?"

"I don't know," Betsy said looking down now at her legs splayed out in front of her on the pavement.

"Here, give me your hand." Serena reached out her hand and helped her mother up. Betsy's hand felt cool and soft and loose-boned. Serena checked her for injury and dirt. She turned her around and brushed off the back of her skirt.

"Why do you think he didn't run?" Betsy said.

"You've scratched your elbow." Serena licked her own fingers and rubbed at the dirt on her mother's elbow.

"Ow."

"Sorry."

"Serena," Betsy said, now standing up straight and looking her daughter directly in the face. "You were going to run him over." She seemed to be searching her daughter's face for something. She said, "When did you become so hard?" Contrary to Betsy's usual approach, this was an actual question and not an accusation. Serena hadn't seen that look on her mother's face in years.

"You were always the kind one," she said, still looking at her carefully. "What's happened?"

Serena looked back at her mother. She saw, with surprise, that Betsy had gotten old. Not old old, but different than what she once was, than what Serena had always known her to be. She looked vulnerable in a way Serena would never have imagined.

"I'm sorry about Eleanor," she said still looking back at her mother. She put a hand on her mother's scratched arm. Betsy stared back at Serena, looking at first merely confused, and then bewildered. She said nothing for a moment.

"But why didn't she call me?" she finally asked Serena. "Why?"

Serena then did something she hadn't done in many years: she put her arms around her mother. It felt funny and awkward, like hugging a stranger at a Christmas party. But she stuck with it.

Betsy began to cry. Sunlight fell through the old elms. "I should call her," Betsy said. "You're right," and she held onto Serena. She hugged her tight for a long time.

"Sweetheart," she said, still hugging her daughter, but calmer now. "I think it's your shampoo."

Serena opened her mouth to speak. She thought of the things she might say. But the appointment was still ahead of them, and the drive home was long.

THE CHANNEL SWIMMER

1

A boy stands by himself in the crowded pub. Toward the back, two women lean their elbows on the table, drinking pints of amber and talking. The boy, still standing alone at the bar, pushes off into the sea of people.

"Can I sit?" He cradles two pints of his own against his chest. "More efficient," he says when asked by one of the women. He places his pints on the table, pushing the untouched one to the centre, as though it were a salt shaker or a bowl of peanuts, a simple thing to be shared.

His body is that of a man's but his face betrays his boyhood. He smells of inexperience, wears a halo of ignorance. He talks, he asks questions they answer. It's true he is twenty-four, but the women see only a boy. This is not immediately apparent to him.

The pub crowd shouts at the five-man band in liquid waves. The boy tries to focus on one woman, then the other. He watches them lift their pints, their lips forming lazy O's against the amber.

"You are," he says, "very attractive women." He gives them a beautiful smile, full of strong young teeth and drunken optimism. They look different, he noticed that when they first walked in. "Cake in a pie shop," he says, still smiling. His eyes are trying to say something seductive, but he's too drunk for it. Besides, he quickly realizes that the women have the upper hand here. They are older than him, by quite a few years, though he hardly believes it. But he knows they are more sober.

The one on the left has doe eyes and a voluptuous mouth. He likes the look. Could be Mediterranean, the boy thinks. The one on the right appeals to his taste for fair-skinned women. Slightly arrogant chin. The way she seems to be observing him frightens him a little, though. Enid. Or maybe it's Emily. No, no, wait, he'll get it. He can't keep their names straight. In fact, he can't remember their names at all. Too late to ask again now.

He talks and talks. Grew up in Birmingham. English mother, Jamaican father. "I don't fit in," he says. He enunciates carefully, to avoid slurring his words. The crowd roars, the band shouts back. The boy looks over his shoulder. "But I fancy a good time," he whispers to the crowd. He closes his eyes and wags his head gently, his mind a slow spin of alcohol.

"My parents wanted me to be a barrister. But I'm a gardener." He opens his eyes and tries to focus. "I imagine you think me stupid," he says. "Because I'm only a gardener." He looks from one woman to the other. Why would they think that? Their gazes are steady. It occurs to him that neither of them is likely to sleep with him.

2

Along the promenade on these angry wind-rapt days, scattered old couples lean back, tucked up in folding chairs and blankets, some of them drinking tea from a thermos, a newspaper obscuring the view. An ageing tableau against multicoloured huts that open up like cardboard boxes blown over in the wind. Few people come to the sea on these days, just the old couples and the occasional middle-aged man, walking his dog into the sunless abyss of a weekday morning.

She's already been here a week before she discovers him. Down by the sea. The Isle of Wight a blight on the horizon, him moving slowly past it in the water.

For that first week she was without him, but after that he is always there. Under the weight of grey sky and muffled afternoon light, she walks the bricked-in streets, heading toward the sea. The streets curve away from each other, petals on a dead orchid. She gets lost most days, but only temporarily. It's just a matter of which roads to choose. Her back to the sea will always lead her to shelter.

A long arc of beach extends up the coastline, a slow exhalation, a relief. Like breathing out smoke. She tosses pebbles into the water, stepping over wooden groynes, the slender brown cracks in the beach that are like fingers reaching into the sea. Gulls perched on the jutting creosoted posts scream into the wind. She has longed for this without even knowing it.

3

An arm reaches out of the sea. One arm, then another, paddling slowly through the water, a slender skein of body trailing through the waves. He kicks, a small white splash, like a large rock dropped into the sea.

The swimmer has a special relationship with the water. He tucks his head between his arms and shuts his eyes against its rough embrace. Breathing is difficult against the unpredictability of thrashing, salty water, but he is working on it. It will be his choice when he stops. The water is freezing, really cold, so that, despite the wetsuit he wears, his body has numbed itself against the icy waves, and he now finds the water, after twenty minutes, almost pleasant. As well, his body is moving on its own, he wouldn't know how to stop it. So he follows it along the coastline, past the wooden posts he has tried and failed to count, past the gulls shouting at him, trying to trick him out of the water. While he swims his mind remains blank, except at the edges, where he sees colours bleeding out into the black flashing waves. His skin is a thin parchment divide between salt water and salt water. He sees the colours as rocks descending, rolling gently like green tumbleweed and kicking up a fine, unlit cloud. A rush of scattering fish. The icy tongue of the water in his ears.

4

The band has started up again. It's really too noisy to talk, but the boy does it anyway. His mind is awash in beer and awful distances, the difficulty of locating what it is he's looking for. He tries to draw a map out of the sticks and stones of words. To find out where his enemies live, and mark it down.

"But I love gardening," he says. "I really do. I look up at the sky at night and think, this is it, this is my life." He has begun to slur a little. "Why the fuck shouldn't I be happy?" The women smile. He can see now that they aren't mocking him. They are on his side. They are outsiders too. Canadians. "I want to travel, you see, I've not been out of England. Well, to Jamaica when I was a baby, but that's not really seeing anything is it?" He kicks one of the women under the table without realizing it. "I want to... I try to learn things, I'm always learning. Reading the dailies, watching the news on the telly." That's right, he's said it just as he meant it. Learning is important. His head feels like it's underwater, fighting a strong current.

No, that sounded ridiculous. He has a growing suspicion these women are a lot brighter than he is. He looks up, and suddenly can think of nothing to say. He fights an urge to get up and run into the crowd. These women are too much for him. "Do you fancy spirits, then? Whiskey and such?"

The band is taking a break between sets. The crowd has closed in around them as if they were rock stars, instead of a sagging cover band still playing at the pubs in their home town. Most of the crowd is well into middle-age. The boy and the two women stand out here. It's true there are three young couples sitting together at a large table near the stage, shouting and drinking along with the crowd. But middle-age will hit them before they know what happened. It will grab them by the throat and pummel them. This is what the boy thinks.

5

This is the town where her father's life began. His first shout into the world. Everything she sees here is loaded with potential significance.

She knows nothing at all about the event, only the circumstances: her grandmother came here to give birth, alone, a stranger seeking anonymity.

In the sea, a man swims. She longs to join him, but, equally, she longs to watch. A wide umbrella of cloud reaches all the way to the unsteady horizon.

The woman thinks of her father's first breath. Sea air.

She climbs the eight steps to the women's lavatory. Inside, a woman with big hair is leaning against one of the sinks, giving an aging man a hand job. The angled mirror in the upper corner of the entrance makes this apparent before anyone has to start apologizing. The industrious pair haven't heard the approach of the woman, the intruder, and she stands now in the entrance, watching. The man looks frail. His eyes are closed, a prayer aimed at the ceiling. He would almost look sad, too, if it weren't for the guttural sounds he is making. The woman with big hair tugs at the man's penis with one hand while with the other she reaches behind her and pumps the soap dispenser. To the woman watching it seems an amazing feat, like rubbing your stomach and patting your head at the same time, or playing Mozart on the piano with both hands. There is a necessary elegance.

6

While he swims, his body has no other need. There is no hunger, no sexual summons, no itch, no urge to defecate. His body has, in fact, almost disappeared. The goggles he is wearing leak, so that when he opens his eyes and glimpses the shore, what he sees is without reference, has no meaning. What he sees, wobbling and murky, could be anything. He's not even sure he is looking in the right direction. Is land to his left or his right? It doesn't matter. It is a conversation with the sea.

As he swims he is so entirely shrouded by the noise of the water slapping against his skull that it achieves the opposite effect: absolute silence. His mind is clear as a bell. He does not think of the job he has just lost. Way down, far below the water's frothing mouth, there is stillness. He pushes along the horizon through the angry slap of waves.

7

The rough wind blowing in off the sea never seems to let up. It whistles and howls in her ears with an urgency that seems both threatening and protective. It won't leave her alone. She has crossed her arms in a protective embrace.

This place is entirely new to her. The pubs, the people, the landscape: all of it novel. And yet everything she sees appears covered in a fine dust. Everything is an artifact from the year of her father's birth.

She stands at the edge of the sea and thinks of her father. When she tries really hard to focus, she imagines a house with loose-mortar joints, standing on an empty, rain-slicked street. With her eyes shut tight, she sees, just barely, her grandmother lying in the humid dark. She opens her eyes so she won't have to look.

When she opens her eyes she sees a man walking towards her on the beach. His head is turned and he is looking toward the water, his grey hair flipped up in the wind. From a distance he embodies her father, his slightly sloping shoulders and the way his long limbs swing comfortable and loose as he walks. She feels a pang of affection.

As he comes closer he turns his head and looks at her. He has a smile that opens out into a grimace. It is the man from the lavatory. She turns away and focuses on the swimmer.

8

This is the band that just won't quit. Against the roar of mutual adoration the boy has finally fallen silent. He stares at his hands cradling one another on the tabletop. He has lost the urge to run. He feels as if he is on the bus, making his way home from the unemployment office.

The two women have turned away from him to watch the band. He has tried to tell them about his life, of how he fills the shallow bowl of his days. He has tried, and they have turned away.

Condensation pools at the base of the boy's pint glass. The room begins to press down on him. He realizes that he is too drunk now for anything.

9

Today her friend is leaving, and she is staying behind. She doesn't know a soul in this town. She will have to manage on her own.

She stares out at the sea and the horizon beyond it. Past the horizon lies a crowded continent, but all she can see is water slapping up against the grey sky like dirty water in an empty fish bowl.

Who swims the channel these days? she wonders. One would have to take it on faith that there is land out there, an entire, enormous continent. Because on setting out a person would see only a vast, watery horizon, an ocean before them with nowhere to alight. She watches the swimmer, alone in the sea. Who would set out under such circumstances?

The water grabs at the swimmer with a lonely urgency, its white, foamy fingers curling into black fists. If she shouted, he would not hear. She watches the swimmer and feels comforted.

10

The swimmer's secret desire is to swim until he arrives somewhere new. He imagines walking up a beach he doesn't know, the weight of the water rushing off of him, like a man newly formed.

But for now, he works to stay afloat. He is lost in the act of blindly moving forward, as if he and the water were dancers, each of them too tired to lead. His body is beginning to weary. He closes his eyes and swims. An ache crawls up his calf, and it feels like a hand gripping him. With his eyes still closed the darkness disorients him, and for a moment he thinks he is swimming at night. On the heels of this thought is a concern that he has come out too far in the dark. He opens his eyes to look for the lights that will direct him to shore, and sees that it is still daytime. This discovery disappoints him. He closes his eyes, but finds that he cannot convince himself to believe in the dark.

11

The swimmer swims. This is all she expects of him. She stands against the wind and watches his steady stroke propel him across the rough waves. She listens carefully for the dull splash as one hand, then the other, breaks the surface of the water. His mouth opens in an exclamation of surprise every time he turns his head.

A cypress-green bicycle with the paint beginning to chip away is locked to a post near the lavatory with a long, loopy cable that looks as if it's ignoring its job. Yet the bike is there every day, and there is no one around to claim it.

She takes out a piece of paper and a pen and sits in the sand. She writes about the things she sees when she looks out at the water. Afterward, back in Canada, she won't be able to say why she wrote it, only that it was an impulse she acted on. She will remember every word.

She folds the piece of paper into quarters and slips it into a slender space on the underside of the bicycle's seat, to be found some time far in the future, or maybe never at all.

You are the channel swimmer, it begins.

12

As he sits staring at his pint glass he makes several interesting discoveries about the physical world around him. He tips his head to the left just for a lark, and he can't believe the weight of it, it would hit the floor like a bowling ball if he let it. He brings his head back upright, and it wobbles back and forth for a moment, as if his neck were a loose spring. He also discovers that he has lost his peripheral vision. He tests this hypothesis by staring at his glass while trying at the same time to observe the movements of the two women. The pub lights reflect off the amber puddle at the bottom of his pint glass. He notices a definite shape to the reflection. He sees the flicker of light and dark as the waitress passes under the lights, her tray held high to avoid the boisterous thrust of arms and moving bodies. She is a mermaid swimming away in the lit pool at the bottom of his pint glass.

The shape in the glass remains. That, he thinks, is a rectangle. Like a shiny piece of paper to write on. The reflection in the glass holds steady. Yes, he thinks, feeling satisfied, as though his job here were done. The rectangle burns onto his retinas like a hot brand. His eyelids drop and still he sees it. The right-angled corners of a piece of paper. He feels buoyed by the folded note in his pocket.

The whole of it takes less than ten seconds, but already he has forgotten to look for the women in his peripheral vision.

While he attends to these thoughts, the pub turns silent. The chatter of the crowd, the guitar solo, the sound of a glass hitting the floor and shattering. He doesn't hear a sound.

INLET

From the top of the steps, the water looked unwholesome. The sun had dipped behind a large, dense cloud that looked a little like an elephant on its knees. There was no breeze at all, and the tiny lake sat before them like a large muddy puddle, the surface a dull and uninviting brown. Cottages and docks were tucked up all around the edge of the lake like desperate children gathered at a third-rate circus.

"You could drink that water," Ber said to reassure Lola. "Seriously." Lola had only remarked on the colour of the water, knowing it didn't necessarily mean anything. His confidence seemed to falter. "Maybe," he said, thinking about it a little more. "You could maybe drink that water." He tugged absently at the waistband of his shorts. "I don't think I would, though."

"Where's the inlet?" Lola asked. There was no sparkle or movement to the water, though she didn't doubt it was clean enough to swim in. This, after all, was cottage country. Ber stared at the water in front of them. He looked vaguely to the left, then to the right. "The inlet?" He wore his swimming trunks hiked halfway up his meager young chest, like an old man with an axe to grind.

It was intimate, but it was also claustrophobic, this little lake. So small there was no room for assumptions. They stood on the dock side by side. Ber was still wearing his shoes and socks. "I'm living the retired life," he said, as they watched a canoe paddle past twenty feet in front of them. It was something he often said, even in the city. He thought it was funny. But it wasn't far from the truth.

Up close the water looked only marginally better. Lola kneeled down to look at it. Beside her Ber did a little vaudeville two-step, then quacked. He raised his chin in the air like he'd come up with something brilliant and quacked again, louder this time, followed by a rapid series of loud, enthusiastic quacks. "Think they'll come?" he said, looking up into the sky expectantly. Lola undid his shoe laces and pretended to tie them together. She leaned closer and sniffed at his shoes, then fell back onto the dock in a dramatic swoon. "I think you need some new Odor Eaters," she said, looking up at him from where she lay.

Ber looked happy for a moment.

"I make no demands," he said, extolling what he thought was one of his virtues. He looked down at her with renewed expectation.

"Why is that good?"

Suddenly he was angry. "Why don't you trust me?" he said, but it was an accusation rather than a question. "We could get married. And..."

"And what?" They'd already had this conversation on the drive up.

"And," Ber looked around him in frustration, "I don't know. We'd be married."

The sun emerged from behind the cloud, and suddenly everything lost its focus. The neighbour's flag drooped on its flagpole.

"Let's swim," Lola said.

Ber flipped his sunglasses down over his eyes and said nothing.

He could look so sullen. Lola stood behind him and rubbed his shoulders. She pressed her face into his back and felt him soften. "Come on," she said, coming around to face him again, "Let's swim for a while, then we'll go fire up the barbeque and open a bottle." She rubbed her hands together and smiled at him. "You can practice your quacking," she added. He smiled back tentatively. They were friends again, for the moment.

Two docks away, a middle-aged man with a deep Florida tan was working on his motorboat. He spotted them and waved. Ber waved back, smiled and nodded several times, hoisted his shorts up even further. "Everyone's always so friendly up here," he said.

"Who's that?"

"I don't know. You just wave back out here."

He reached for her index finger and fondled it for a moment. "People like to keep to themselves." Two ducks came into view overhead and dove towards the lake, flapping and skidding onto the surface of the water. Ber raised his eyebrows at Lola and shook his finger at the ducks wildly, like a demented old man. "It worked!" he said.

Lola was still looking at the neighbour. "He looks like the guy who does the news on TV," she said. Ber suddenly looked surprised, and turned his head towards the man with the Florida tan. "Oh yeah," he said. "It *is* the guy who does the news. My parents go over there for barbeques." He looked back at the ducks. "Ap-parent-ly." He did another little two-step.

"I forgot my towel," Ber said, doing something with his face that was halfway between a smile and a grimace. The sound of someone hammering echoed across the little lake. Some industrious neighbour was building an addition onto their cottage. Lola thought it could be fun to paddle across and offer to help for a couple of hours, then afterward sit and drink beer with them by the lake, pointing back to where they stood now and saying, Look, that's where we are. But Ber would never want to do that. She waited, looking out toward the sound. Ber looked at the water without making a move toward the house. He shifted his weight to one leg, while giving the other one a tentative shake, pantomiming pain from when he had banged his foot on the door stoop earlier that morning.

"Want me to get it for you?" Lola said, still looking out across the lake.

"No, no, of course not," he said, giving his foot another slight shake and twisting his face into a minor grimace.

"I'll get it," she said, and turned to look at him briefly. He gave her a guilty smile.

"Thank you!" he shouted after her as she headed back up the hill toward the house.

The house had that genteel cottagey feel, all wood and windows, with carved ducks on the side tables and floor-to-ceiling windows looking out over the lake. Boating magazines were laid out on the coffee table beside a thick glass bowl filled with coloured marbles. The house had a funny smell.

Two large, pink Post-It notes on the fridge bore one of the few living signs of Ber's parents. It was a list: a list of tasks to be performed while Ber and Lola were up there. *Hi kids!* it said at the top. Ber's mother was responsible for this.

It wasn't simply a list of things that needed doing, but ways that regular things were meant to be done. *Double-bag the garbage!* was the first one. *Don't leave anything perishable in the refrigerator!* came next. The third one was interesting. *Don't put any utensils in the toaster!!!* Lola could only assume that Ber's mother thought a) that Ber was still nine years old; or b) that he was an idiot. It was depressing to see such a bald lack of faith in a son. Lola had read it aloud in disbelief when they'd arrived, but Ber seemed unperturbed by it. "She means well," was all he'd said.

The Post-It list was an interesting artifact, the kind of thing you could take to a psychoanalyst and have him tell you where your life had gone off track. In fact, Lola herself could slip it in her bag and show it to a shrink. She could have him read it like tea leaves in the bottom of a cup, tell her what a future with Ber would hold.

She opened the fridge door absently. It was full of the food they'd brought, but also the stuff that Ber knew she loved. He had run in to the country store on their way up here to grab a newspaper, and emerged with a paper grocery bag full of fancy cheeses and artichokes, black olives and Alphaghettis, two things of Jiffy Pop and a bottle of cheap bourbon to make up for the one she'd forgotten to pack. She looked at the bourbon sitting on the counter. As the fridge door swung shut, she caught the words *Lock the door!* down at the bottom of the second Post-It. She reached for the bourbon and drank it straight from the bottle.

Ber's painting lay on the kitchen table. He'd started it that morning in a fit of enthusiasm. It was the starkest thing she had ever seen. Next to the painting lay all his paint things, nothing closed up properly, the brushes tipped out of the murky dish of water and onto the wood of the table. The chair cushion had fallen onto the floor. She picked up a brush and added a stroke of blue to the water. She painted a tree onto the horizon, suggesting land where there had only been a wide-open expanse of ocean that went on and on. She added another tree, and a stick man standing beneath it. She added a small platform of land. It was done before she could stop herself.

In searching for Ber's towel, Lola discovered a turquoise bag of moist wipes sitting on the floor in the front entrance. This was where Ber had unwittingly dropped them.

"I can't find them," she'd called to him from outside the bathroom door the evening before. "Take a shower if you can't manage to clean yourself the old-fashioned way."

"But I need them," he'd whined through the door.

"You'll manage."

She heard muffled sounds of movement through the door.

"My ass is my bread and butter!" he shouted.

"Funny," she shouted back. "What do you want from me? I can hose you down if you'd like."

She'd thought he was making a joke of it, but he didn't talk to her for a good twenty minutes after emerging from the bathroom.

She was still carrying the bourbon around. She took another swig and put it down on the table. Looking out the big window, she could just make out Ber from here, standing motionless down on the dock. It was like looking at a photograph. She tried to imagine him gone from her life. She managed it, but it hurt. She stripped off her clothes and dropped them on the floor. She didn't want to be alone in this house anymore.

From the balcony overlooking the lake, Lola called to Ber. "Anyone in sight?" Standing way down on the dock, pale-skinned with his shoe laces undone, dwarfed by the distance between them, Ber did a quick scan then shook his head. A breeze had come up, and the lake was rallying. It sparkled a little in the sunshine.

Lola jogged down the steps with Ber's towel wrapped around her. As she got closer to the dock she picked up speed. When she hit the dock, she dropped the towel.

"It has to be done!" she shouted, streaking past Ber and cannonballing into the water.

The water was icy. She hadn't expected that. Her skin burned for a few moments, before it began to numb.

Ber was laughing. She watched him. When she made him laugh, she was happy.

"It's okay," she said, gasping a little as she spoke, her body trying to adjust to the cold. "It's just the first shock" — she could hardly catch her breath — "that hurts."

Ber paced the dock like a caged dog. She knew it was hard for him. But she wanted him to try.

"Just come in," she called, "come in with me, and we'll swim." She turned in the water, her hands like the oars of a small craft moving her roughly, but pointing her in the right direction. She raised a hand out of the water, causing the rest of her to sink a little. She was determined to try. "There," she said pointing across the little lake. "We'll swim to that cluster of trees, and see what we find."

"You'll find another dock just like this one," Ber said, "and people who don't want you on their property, particularly if you're naked."

Lola continued to tread water in front of the dock. She was getting cold, and would soon need to either start swimming or get out. "Maybe we'll find the inlet," she said, looking across the lake. She didn't want to get out.

Ber was frustrated with her. His face had crumpled in on itself like a wounded animal's, and she could see that he was unhappy.

He looked down at her treading water in front of the dock. "We could go to Vegas," he said. "We could." But still, the water was too cold, and he wouldn't come in.

TEN-CENT PACKS

Sender's house smells faintly of urine. It's not from his dog Milo, but is the smell of an anxious child, of warm pee on unwashed trousers.

"Mona was my life," he says, "but I'll never give Milo back." He grips Milo against his chest. Milo looks sedated, her head drooping in Sender's arms and her back legs sprawling out across his lap. This is a rare moment for Milo, who is normally, happily, out of control.

On the days when I entertain Milo, we go out to my backyard and play. She has become quite fond of the sprinkler. I like to sit beneath the willow tree and throw sticks and assorted items for her to chase. This morning she brought me a sneaker that I suspect belonged to Mona. She leapt back and forth through the sprinkler with it several times before depositing it at my feet. We can do this sort of thing for hours. I am easily mesmerized by her energy, and by the smells that emanate from the garden, and my skin, when either is exposed to the summer sun.

Things get left undone in Sender's house. The dishes are growing mold in the sink and his tub is full of dirty clothes, that are, he tells me in his defense, soaking. Once in a while he changes the water and, occasionally, I can make out a slight froth around the outer edges, which suggests he has even added soap.

Sender takes off his shoe and places his foot in the water. "Why do you stay?" he asks me. His foot moves vigorously through the murk of wet fabric, swishing it back and forth in one dark clump with a pause that is a fraction of a second longer on the back stroke. If I focus on his body and edit out the fact of the tub, the movement he's engaged in suggests something else entirely, like kicking at the pavement to get a skateboard up a hill.

"Why do you?" I ask back. But I know the answer already.

Sender is always saying she'll come back. I never talked to Mona, I knew her only by her hat, a broad, flat, floppy thing, meant for a 1940s beach. I could see it over the fence. She wore it with Jackie O's while sunbathing out in their backyard, or packing the trunk of her new lover's car with the household appliances that Sender had given her at Christmases and birthdays.

The only reason I started talking to Sender at all was because he came to my door one day covered in plaster and smelling remotely of piss, asking to borrow my garden hose. We walked around the side of the house, and I started to unscrew the hose from the back faucet.

"No no," he said, "it'll only take a second." He took off his shirt and dropped it in the grass, then turned on the hose and held it over his head. His shoulders and back were sunburnt and streaked with plaster. It was easy to see what his work was. And I already knew the essential thing about him, everyone on the street did. He was the one whose dog ripped open garbage bags put out the night before early-morning pickup. This meant we all had to get up extra-early if we didn't want our trash spread out across the pavement and consequently rejected by the garbage collectors.

"Why," I asked, confused by his presence in my yard, "don't you use your own?" He pulled the front of his shorts open and stuck the hose inside.

"My dog chewed through it," he said. His shorts sprang outwards like an inflatable ring. I liked the look of him, lost somewhere in his thirties, clearly against his will. He looked at me, unsmiling, then pulled the hose out of his shorts and shut off the faucet. He resembled a sea otter: black eyes, hair plastered to his head and running dark and slick to his shoulders, a skinny glistening line of fine black hair merging down his chest and stomach.

"Come and meet her," he said.

Late-August mowers scream up and down the lawns. Frequently these days I find myself in the pantry staring at all the canned food I've been stockpiling since I arrived. I don't know why I do it. The stockpiling, I mean. Peas and corn and beans of all varieties, tomato paste, an endless selection of soups and raviolis, bamboo shoots, carrots, evaporated milk. Asparagus tips and clam chowder. Tinned curries and water chestnuts. Recently my head has been feeling as though it is being pressed in upon, especially with the roar of miniature motors outside. But I've discovered that if I shut the pantry door behind me and stand at the back the noise is reduced to a single, remote hum. During these periods, I've found myself mentally planning the menu for my winter meals. This afternoon I'm doing February. Nearly an hour passes before I come out again. These sorts of things are without consequence, which is one of the benefits of living alone.

Another good thing about living alone is that when the telephone rings I don't have to answer it. I got rid of the answering machine a while ago, too much emotive clutter. I had to consider the fact of my mother, who is out there and doing her best to tap me for energy, which, when she succeeds, leaves me wilted for days.

In the garden the corn is growing tall, though I've come to suspect that it isn't corn at all. Stunted arms and formless heads, protective husks around baby ears that are gathering in size like tumors. They are grouped out back and looming as the house grows smaller. An impending riot. It's alarming, really. I've explained it to Sender but he prefers to discuss the question of how many times a person can be randomly struck by lightning before permanent internal damage becomes inevitable.

"Who do you know who has been struck even once?" I've asked him this before.

"That isn't the point," is all he ever says. But the corn still looms large and something will have to be done.

The floors of my tiny house creak and tremble when I walk, so I've taken to shuffling, careful not to move too fast. My grandmother's photos are still on the mantle, though I've long gone through the contents of her liquor cabinet. It was stocked extraordinarily well, with backups hidden in the drawers beneath. Everything was in old, cut-glass decanters, and it took me a while to remember what was what.

I moved into the house when she got ill, a temporary measure six months ago, and remained after she died. It felt too sad to leave the house empty. None of my plans fit anymore, anyway.

Sender is always upset these days, and his smell is getting stronger. I do the best I can to calm him. On the afternoons he isn't working he sits inside and watches daytime dramas while Milo chases cars up and down the street. He likes to tell me who is deceiving who. I make him tuna casseroles and bring them over to cover the smell.

I brought my grandmother soup and tea for the four weeks before she disappeared, and she took to telling me that my father had been an irresponsible man. Every day she sank further into her pillows. I did what I could for her, which wasn't much. I breathed in the last of her life with her.

Her room was filthy and I tried to clean it, but she'd wake up every time and catch me. She insisted she didn't want it clean. Like holding one's breath, she said out of the blue. She didn't talk much toward the end, though she had taken to waving her hand around meekly and saying, "Take it all, take it all. You know, you look just like your mother." She knew that was a low blow. I looked around the room. There was really nothing to take. But I said nothing, just brought her more tea. There was no reason to hurt her feelings.

The corn smells brittle and sweet, yet thick, like a throat that needs to be cleared. I catch the scent of it most often at night and it makes me wonder what I will do when the time arrives to harvest it. There are fourteen stalks, and they were unthinkingly planted to the south of the tomatoes so that the tomatoes remain shrunken and pale, a little like rotted golf balls, even though it is late in the season. I never thought any of it would grow, the seeds had been sitting in my grandmother's drawer since I don't know when. The packets said *10¢*.

Mona called Sender last night while he was out playing poker and left a message on his answering machine. Milo had been left behind, banished from the group for unruly behaviour. I heard her bark several times through the open window, muffled woofs of excitement. She must have recognized Mona's voice.

Mona's message said she wanted Milo back, and would be coming for her some time soon.

Sender refuses to talk about it. Whenever I bring it up he just calls Milo over and talks gibberish to her, then flips her on her back and scratches her armpits. I don't know how he will manage.

Mrs. Goody's budgie escaped last week, flew right out the back door and into the warm sunlight. She came loping out after it, shouting. The door had been left open for the breeze and the last time she had looked the bird was secure, hanging sideways from one of the curtains in the kitchen. She'd been cleaning its cage and hadn't thought of escape. She said she liked to let it have a stretch every now and again. Sender mentioned the lightning and said it would never survive. But I was thinking more along the lines of Milo. We searched Mrs. Goody's yard and discovered the budgie in the birch tree at the back of the house. We tried everything, but it just ignored us. Sender offered to build it a birdhouse so it would have somewhere safe to go. Mrs. Goody was smiling with relief and wouldn't stop touching his arm after that.

She has left her back door open wide every night since, hoping her budgie will retrace its path, but I suspect it won't be coming back. The nights are growing cold and already smell heavily of autumn.

"You can't smell corn while it's still on the stalk," Sender finally said to me. We were sitting in his backyard watching Mrs. Goody hang out her laundry and eating popsicles he'd bought from the ice cream truck. I could tell that he'd wanted to say this for some time.

"You don't smell it?" I asked.

He sucked on his popsicle. "What, you do?" Then he repeated his initial remark about the corn. I wondered about this, then decided to dismiss it.

"What do you know about corn," I said. He just sucked at his popsicle and watched Mrs. Goody.

He hasn't brought it up again, but I've noticed

that recently he becomes impatient whenever I mention the garden.

During the days I wander around the house, looking at the dusty picture frames on the walls, the fading furniture, the yellowing walls themselves. I don't feel compelled to touch them, to alter them in any way. Yet depending on the day, there are certain rooms I'm loath to enter. Sometimes it's my grandmother's room, sometimes my own. But each time I wander I discover something new. Yesterday I realized that my grandmother's smell is growing faint, and a different one is taking over. I thought the rugs would be the best place to confirm this, but then found that I couldn't go near my own room. The rug by the couch was just like spring grass on my bare hands and the tops of my feet, so soft that there was no need for my bed anyway. I lay right down and went to sleep on the living room floor.

This morning when I woke up I spotted a glove under the couch that I hadn't seen before. I tried to concentrate on seeing it on my grandmother's hand but found that I couldn't remember what she looked like.

Milo has disappeared. She does this every so often, takes off without warning then returns a few days later stinking of whatever dead thing she has found to roll in. Sender has gotten used to it, he says, and doesn't bother to worry, but I've see him wandering around in strange places with Milo's unused leash sticking out of his back pocket.

I've noticed Sender's attic window recently, opened wide at night, and when I asked him about it, he said that he doesn't have an attic. But there it is, clear as day, a small window just below the eaves of his house. When I pointed it out to him he looked perplexed, then told me I knew nothing about house construction.

I first saw it open when I got up to pee one night, after tossing and turning over dreams that had gone wrong. Sender was in them. He had come over to fix the clock in the kitchen for me, but instead he was nailing my grandmother to a chair. It must have been 4 AM. I've seen the window open twice again since, but Sender insists that I'm confusing dreams with reality.

Sender never mentions Mona anymore, and he never built the birdhouse he promised Mrs. Goody. She has grown visibly hostile towards him and frowns severely whenever she sees him across the hedge. The days lately have been cloudy, sombre, and disconcertingly still, and Sender has been acting irrational and moody. When I asked him about the birdhouse he snapped at me and said that he had only suggested it as a way of consoling her. I thought that was particularly cruel. He said I was full of shit, and since then we haven't talked much, though mainly because he has chosen to retreat into the recesses of his house, not to be disturbed.

This afternoon I found a letter in my mother's handwriting. It took me a minute to get past the strange feeling of familiarity. It's written in pencil and addressed to my grandmother, fifteen years ago, and is lonely and rambling, revealing the insignificant details of her days. When I continued looking through the drawer where I found it, I came across a half-page reply, unsent. *One makes one's own bed*, it begins.

The smell of the corn is so intense tonight that it has woken me from pleasant dreams of Mrs. Goody's budgie riding on Milo's back through the apple groves where Sender takes her on occasion to run. I could picture it perfectly when I first woke up, the colours of the budgie as it held on tight while Milo galloped as fast as she could, her ears flowing back against the breeze. But the smell of the corn is so strong that the dream is already being blotted out, and I'm beginning to feel ill at ease. When I go downstairs and out into the backyard, the smell mixes with the night air and quickly becomes suffocating. The anemic tomatoes bend curiously over the corn, because the corn is no longer standing. My feet bleed from stepping across broken stalks.

Sender came to the door this morning covered in dried plaster and no shirt. He wanted to tell me that he'd found Milo, but he went on about the ignition in his truck for a while before he was able to say what he meant. While he talked, he jiggled the knocker on my door, asked if I had a screwdriver so he could tighten it up for me. I told him to leave it alone.

"I believe in signs," he said, watching his toe through the hole in his shoe. Sender didn't want to come in and sit down, he said he had to get back to work, but he wanted me to come with him and see. "Just ten minutes," he said, and I got in his truck. The weather was starting to turn, the air shifted around and was growing cool. We drove in silence along the back roads through the apple trees, to the lot where he'd found his dog.

"I ran Milo here every day," he said with nostalgia as we got out, which, strictly speaking, wasn't true. She was under a tree, bailing twine twisted around her neck and the flies humming around her like cigarette smoke. Her eyes were still open but her head had already begun to decompose, making it hard to know for sure what was what. The wind was picking up and gusting through the apple trees. Sender crouched down to look at Milo, with whom he had spent so much time. A thick crust of black that must have been vomit lay beside her. Sender put his hand out and scratched behind her ears, and a smell came up that was too much, made me snap my head back and turn away. Sender pulled his hand back, holding it like a glass paperweight in the air between us. I noticed his face receding white, merging with the plaster on his hands.

A few drops fell, not enough warning, and then it was coming down in sheets.

"It's Mona," he said. "She wanted too much." He snapped the twine off the dog's neck as the rain swept down his nose, his chin, dripped from the overexposed ends of him. It made me weary, looking at Sender with his dog lying there rotting in front of him and the rain coming down. I leaned my head on his shoulder. There was nothing I could say, I knew what he had done. At least the rain was driving the flies away.

If Mrs. Goody's budgie is still alive, it won't be after this rain storm. I picture it in the birch tree huddled beneath scant leaves. I imagine it alone and calling out in budgie cries, for comfort.

The apple trees are dropping fruit. Sender places his hand in the bare, damp space behind my bent knee. His fingers stink from scratching Milo. The corn has been felled, razed to the ground. It was, possibly, an act of empathy, but I know it is time that I left. We lean back on slow-rotting apples and the rain comes down. Yet when I place my chin on Sender's plaster-streaked chest the smells get all mixed up. The evidence is there, and he has left his fingerprints all over the back of my knee.

SEVEN OPENINGS OF THE HEAD

"I don't think you understand," he said. We were sitting on a bench at the crest of the hill, still wearing our cross-country skis. It was awkward, there was no way for argumentative leg crossing, but we were both lazy in the same way. I wasn't clear how we were going to get up from the bench. Stand up and push off I suppose. There was a full moon overhead, and the night was bright and cold, the air sharp as the edge of a tin can.

"What? What don't I understand?" I stood up, then sat down again, unwilling to expose myself just at that moment. I knew what I didn't understand. He was right in a certain way. I didn't. I hated my own ignorance.

I pulled the flask out of my pocket and took a swig without offering it first. Then I held it in my lap until he had to ask for it by holding his hand out and waggling his mitten at me. It was an impotent form of protest, but I couldn't help myself.

He'd been telling me about an acquaintance of his, a man he used to know way back, who had been in a car accident over the holidays and was now paralyzed. "Do me in if that ever happens to me," he'd said. It upset me more than it ought to have. I'd been feeling strangely out of sorts all day.

He took a swig and looked up at the moon. "It's so bright," he said, "you can't see the stars."

I wanted another drink from the flask but wasn't about to ask for it back. "So now you resent the moon?"

From where we sat we could see the frozen-over lake, still and icy. Snow dunes that had been intricately chiselled by driving winter winds were now sparkling like a frozen desert under the bright path of the moon. Behind us in the woods, trees moaned and creaked, brittle dormant life in the February night.

"Why does it bother you so much?" He was calm, staring at the moon the way you stare at a campfire.

"I don't know," I said, and somehow his asking diffused things a little.

"I wonder," I said after a time, "if animals get depressed in the winter the way people do."

"No," he said. "Animals don't get depressed."

"Sure they do. Look at animals in a zoo."

"That's different."

"What about elephants when they lose a family member?"

"That's mourning."

From where we were sitting I could see three naked maples and a stand of silver birch that were clearly ailing. Maybe it was a trick of the moonlight, and the dark mountain rising up behind them, giving healthy, winter-bare trees the tint of decay. Together they leaned in and up toward the sky like a lonely, crumbling castle. Yet it was a perfect night, a night that felt like it belonged to itself. He was right about the moon. It wiped out the stars.

"My mother has become morbid," I said. "She was telling me this morning about this woman in her seventies who died forty-eight days after her husband."

"It happens all the time," he said.

"I don't suppose that makes it any less tragic."

"Death like that isn't tragic. They'd both already lived full lives."

"That's easy to say when you still have a long life ahead of you," I said. "People get left behind. It doesn't seem right."

He took a drink and said, "Why is this a surprise to you?" then handed me the flask.

Everything felt sharp and in focus in a peculiar way. When he reached over with both of his hands and pulled my scarf up over my nose, his eyes and his attention carefully focused, I experienced a sensation so intense it felt like I'd been jabbed with a stick. The moonlight reflected off the snow and in that light his face looked ageless. He became black and white, a living photograph. His nostrils flared as he breathed in the cold night air, and a moment later I watched his breath escape through his mouth in huffs of hot vapour. I thought, I must keep you safe, and felt a slight spasm in my stomach.

"I can hear you breathing," he said to me. "You sound like you're asleep."

"Maybe I am," I said, suddenly made aware of the shallow breaths of cold air I was pulling in and the hot, used-up breaths I was forcing out through my scarf.

"Your eyes are open," he said. "So you must be thinking. You make a lot of noise when you think."

"Is that true?"

"Yes it is," he said.

"Well, you whistle through your nose when you read."

"What were you thinking about?"

"I was thinking about my mother," I lied, because I'd been thinking about him, and it occurred to me that life offers itself up to you, glittering and huge, then somewhere down the line takes it all back.

"What about her?" he asked.

"She's turning seventy next week."

"Really?"

"Yeah."

"That's surprising," he said, and looked back up at the moon.

"I don't know how it happened." The thought that I hadn't really been paying attention frightened me.

After a time, we got up from the bench and pushed off into the snow. We needed to move, we were both getting cold. We fell into stride, moving fast across the dense, crystalline surface. The night was perfect for skiing. The moon cast long shadows the way streetlamps do, but these were static and stricken and beautiful. As we skied, *shush-shushing* along in the quiet midnight, our shadows followed alongside us. Once we'd been moving for a bit, I warmed up again. I thought of what it must have been like, centuries before, to move through the winter forests of an unknown continent, not knowing where you were going, or what lay ahead. Not knowing how to find your way back. I tried to imagine it, and for a moment I successfully managed to disorient myself so that the forest looked utterly unfamiliar. I experienced an odd, vertiginous feeling. Like jumping off a cliff. For a moment it was thrilling. Then fear, like a sharpened branch, pressed into my chest.

Off in the distance we heard barking, and then the faint voice of a man calling to his dog. The dog continued to bark, and he was obviously running through the woods, because the barking got closer, then headed off in the other direction. The man's voice called out again, no closer than before, then everything went quiet again.

We both stopped to listen. "Probably chasing a fox," he said, looking off in the direction of the barking.

"Do foxes run at night?" I asked, because in that moment I couldn't remember.

"Sure," he said, looking at me closely. "They're like vampires." As he turned his head a thick spiral of vapour curled up from his mouth like an exiting genie. "They sleep at dawn." He looked at me but the moon was directly above him and all I could see was the outline of his head, the dark recesses where his eyes were located, the craggy outline of his fighter's nose.

"The living dead," I said for no reason, and shivered. The wind was picking up, and we had slowed, hanging back, not skiing fast enough anymore to escape the cold. I looked up, hoping now for the stars, but got only a blinding glare. I sighed, and he must have taken it as some sort of cue, because he penguin-stepped backwards until he was standing beside me. He reached his arms around me in a bear hug, then pulled his head back awkwardly and looked me in the eyes.

"You look like the day I met you," he said.

I didn't have a clue what he was talking about. "Unh huh," I said, to hide my confusion.

"And you'll still look that way to me even after everything has started to sag and you've completely lost your mind."

"How romantic," I said. "Thanks."

"Now stop dwelling on shit you can't change," he said, still holding onto me. With his face beside mine, he looked out at the snowy landscape, as if it were a frozen ocean and he were locked in its icy grip. His fortieth birthday was in two days. He looked on this fact as some sort of dirty trick that had been played on him. He'd had plenty of warning, but somehow he hadn't really seen it coming. Neither of us had.

"You're right," I said, not entirely feeling it. I kissed his cheek and there was no heat to it, only a damp, clinging cold that made me press my own cheek against it to warm it up. He was vulnerable to frostbite. His cheeks, his nose, his ears had all been touched. "Let's ski to the point," I said into his cheek. Then I kissed his lips, and they were icy too.

I tried to remember if foxes were solitary but my memory was failing me from lack of sleep. I couldn't sleep before dawn these days, lying awake alone in the dark. I could picture different foxes standing still and solitary on a ridge, but these were images from nature scenes on television and I wasn't prepared to trust them.

"We could read by this light," I said, amazed by the brightness of the moon and the reflecting snow. "I bet we could even read newsprint."

"Do you think we could read the obituaries?" He didn't turn his head around when he spoke.

"I could certainly write yours if you'd like," I said, and poked him with my ski pole.

We stopped at the edge of the forest. "Flask,"

he said like a surgeon, and held out his thick, mittened hand. We stood and drank, a silent ritual before entering the dark woods.

"Pull down your flaps," I said, "the wind is picking up." He dutifully pulled his earflaps down over his ears.

The woods were only marginally darker. The moon blazed through the bare treetops like a searchlight from a bridge. The snow sparkled, glinting and winking like a calm river. The regular *shush, shush* of our skis gliding across the snow sounded like the flapping wings of a giant solitary bird.

The wind was definitely picking up, and the woods began to creak and shudder. The shadows cast by the trees, so still before, now waved and bent across the snowy floor, dark and chaotic.

We had skied these woods at night before, never taking exactly the same path, but knowing the signposts: rocks with peculiar shapes and rotten trees bent in half, a stand of young balsam, a big, old pine with a huge section of branches missing from its midsection. We skied now into the wind, our heads down, and after a while I realized he had taken us off in a different direction. When I called ahead to him through the wind, he half-turned his head and shouted, "We can loop back home this way." He weaved ahead of me through the trees and I did my best to keep up. After a bit, I caught up to him standing by a rock face.

"Where's your hat?" I asked.

"I don't know. I was sweating so I took it off, just for a minute. I thought I put it in my pocket."

His dark hair clung to his skull, frozen with sweat. He looked so brittle in the cold, naked without his hat.

"We have to find it," I said, looking now at the blood-red tips of his ears.

I'm sure he protested, but I couldn't hear it against the wind. I flipped my skis up and around and headed off the way we'd come. "Stay by the rock," I shouted over my shoulder. "I'll be right back." I looked briefly at him, standing with his hands over his ears like a frozen chimp that refuses to hear.

I skied back a quarter mile before realizing the futility of it. The wind would have swept away anything lying on the surface of the snow. I would never find it, no matter how hard I looked. For some reason, the thought of it shook me.

I didn't know this part of the woods. Which way is home? I thought. I didn't look up. I turned around and headed back to the rock face as fast as I could.

When I got back to the rock, I couldn't find him, and for a moment I panicked, thinking he'd gone ahead, unprotected and exposed. I circled around to the other side of the rock then saw his skis standing in the snow.

"Where are you?" I shouted.

"In here," he shouted back. I followed his voice past a seam in the rock that opened into a deep recess. "In here," he said again, and I headed toward his voice, into the dark shadows of a shallow cave.

I located him by the sound of his movements. He was shifting over to make room for me.

"Out of the wind," he said, his shoulder pressing up firmly against mine.

"I couldn't find it," I said, and felt oddly, yet profoundly, that I had failed him. "Are you freezing?" I took off my mittens and reached out toward him, feeling my way around until I had his face in my hands, like a child seeking an audience. "You're going to get frostbite," I said feeling the cold seeping out of his cheeks, nose, ears, and lips, into my warm hands. I pulled my arms into my sleeves, backing out of my clothes like a creature from its shell. I went all the way in until my hands brushed against my naked stomach, and then I began to peel off that innermost layer of thermal wear.

"Here," I said, rolling and folding the warm shirt then reaching up to wrap it around his ears and head. He pulled away from me.

"What are you doing?" he said, knowing the answer already.

"Don't be stupid," I said reaching out again for his head. "My hands are freezing, stop moving." I knew this would make him hold still.

"You need your undershirt," he muttered, "your jacket is crappy." He didn't quite seem to be addressing me. "You've got a crappy little jacket that won't keep you warm. Why? Because you're a cheapskate, that's why. Out in the middle of the woods in a shitty little spring jacket. And now you're a martyr, taking off your one warm layer so I don't get cold ears."

"Shut up," I said. "I'm not a martyr. You have no idea. I just need to keep you close tonight." The warmth had disappeared from my shirt while we argued. "Besides, it's too late now. That trick only works in one direction."

"What trick?" he looked at me suspiciously, as if I were speaking in code.

"With the shirt."

So he sat still for me, and I lovingly wrapped his head in the cotton shirt, placing the body of the shirt over the top of his skull, the heat from his head infusing it with warmth, then twisting and wrapping the arms across the front of his forehead, the knot of fabric like a misshapen amulet, then back firmly over his ears and tying them together at the back. At one point he said, "I can smell you perfectly," and smiled, but his eyes remained closed the entire time. I pulled the knot snug at the back, leaning toward him in a rough embrace. I sat back to look at my handiwork.

"You look like Tutankhamen. With a drippy nose," I said. He opened his eyes, and looked at me with a slightly glazed look, as if he'd been asleep. "Thanks," he said. He reached into his pocket for his handkerchief.

"Is it warm enough?"

"Is this what it feels like after a head injury?" he said. "It feels like necrosis is about to set in."

I reached behind him and loosened it up.

"Better?"

"Much better." He reached up and touched his head. "Do I look jaunty?"

I smiled, a smile he may or may not have been able to see, and looked at his shadowy black and white self.

We sat in the mouth of the cave until the wind died down a bit. We were both enjoying the feeling of being out in the woods at night. "It's like we're winter camping in here," he said, snuggling up against me.

I couldn't shake the unwieldy feeling of being somewhere I'd never been before.

I thought of all the travelling I did as a child with my family, down long, empty highways, my mother singing in the front seat. Some songs she sang for us, and others just for herself. I never paid attention to where we were.

My mother would be seventy. But she would live a long time still.

I reached for his hand. "Which way is home," I asked.

He held my hand and squeezed it. Instead of

answering, he whispered, "Look." I turned to look out at the woods.

Out on the snow a fox stood perfectly still, looking in our direction, listening.

The wind shifted, gusting for a moment into the place where we squatted. A bolt of cold shot through my chest. The fox stood for a moment longer, knowing we were there, somewhere, but unwilling to leave without knowing whether we were food or foe.

"We're here," I whispered to the fox. And, seeming to hear me, he picked up and ran.

TRITON AND TEX

Artie was saying, "Give me the keys, give me the keys," when Helen saw that the door was already standing wide open. She was thinking, What for? but knew that he wanted to lock the house against further intrusion. It made no sense, the place had already been stripped, but she understood the shaky feeling, the need to cover up. A train blasted its whistle at the intersection half a mile down the road. "Fucking Christ," Artie said, and Helen thought, Yes, yes, nothing to do but go. Then she saw that it was aimed at her. After a moment she dug into her pockets. Her fingers touched cold metal. She pulled out the keys and handed them to Artie. He stood framed in the doorway looking inward with the keys in his hand. Helen noted that the back of his jacket had a streak of bird shit on it, and that his hair had begun to thin a little on top. She looked at the keys in his hand, looked at the door standing open. The house had been transformed before her eyes into a hostile entity. The train roared past. "Unlucky," Artie said, and stepped into the house.

Helen turned to watch the train pass on the opposite side of the road. The names offered no indication of points of origin. The cars used to have *Alberta Wheat* or *BC Lumber* painted on them, giving her a feeling of size, the tracks stretching all the way across the country. But Helen hadn't seen those trains lately. Only these unidentifiable ones, that gave her the feeling that she had been left behind. She wondered where this train was going, aware of the sound of Artie's boots clumping from room to room upstairs. The last car disappeared down the track and a moment later Artie's footsteps stopped. She heard him say, "Who am I talking to?" then continue to check each room, taking account of what they had lost.

Making tea became difficult for Helen, who was used to plugging in the kettle then sitting in her old rocking chair by the porch door to wait. Hemmed in by the refrigerator on one side and the wall on the other, doing nothing in anticipation of a certainty gave her a strange pleasure. The wait was calming, helped her over the hump of 4 PM. But the chair had been stolen, and she found herself pacing the house, critical. The furniture was decrepit, the lampshades yellowed. The kitchen got the afternoon sun, but that only made things worse. The table and chairs, the bottled spices over the stove, the cupboards full of food. Each remained poised and still, and kept its distance. Even the glasses and mugs and plates, all empty, clean, and waiting. Everything threatened. Out back the yard was winter-ravaged, with mounds of shrinking snow and moldy leaves and a garden that was empty.

There was the shriek of a crow. It flew into view, dropped down toward the dead grass then climbed again into the air without appearing to lose speed. The crows were so much bigger than they had been in her youth, they unsettled her whenever she saw them up close, perched aggressively on the edge of public trash cans, leaning in and ripping at discarded paper plates and crumpled chip bags. There was a ferocity to them, they were scavengers who had swelled in physical size on the satisfaction of abandoned picnics.

Helen was cold; she shivered. She headed back into the kitchen to check on the kettle and found, as she often did these days, that she had forgotten to plug it in.

The sun hit the floorboards, drew a line up to the door. Helen awoke to the sound of a train passing. The carpet had had to be taken up, and she lay stretched out in a chair by the window. The living room felt empty, even though only the carpet and the television were missing. Artie was still upset about the TV going.

"What do you expect?" Helen had said standing in the bedroom doorway one evening. She looked at Artie lying on top of the covers flipping the tongue of his belt back and forth.

"But Christ, why the television?" he said. "Couldn't they have broken in last month?" In the time since the robbery the conversations between them had felt like acting to Helen. There had been so many rehearsals that the words meant nothing.

"It was one of the few valuable things in the place," Helen said, thinking of her computer and all her work lost. "Of course they were going to take it." Artie looked annoyed but said nothing. He had given away his small black-and-white when he'd bought the new one, and was suffering now from withdrawal. Helen stopped looking at Artie and focused on the black pane in the window beyond him. A moment later the house began to shiver.

"Train," Helen said quietly, and they both listened in silence until it had passed and the house was still again.

"I'm going over to Tom and what's-her-name's." Artie swung off the bed and tucked in his shirt.

"Katia," Helen offered.

"Yeah," Artie said, and galloped down the stairs.

Helen stretched out in the chair and sat up, the sunlight spreading across her lap like a quilt. Her house had been broken into, someone had stepped uninvited into a corner of her life and made off with her belief in escape. She must have been dreaming it. No one owes me anything, she thought. The thought of Artie squeezed itself around her like a jacket that was too tight in the shoulders.

She was still in the chair by the window, trying to get some reading done, when he floated by like a bird, or an empty bag on the breeze. A man with a white baseball cap passed against a backdrop of skeletal trees and empty track, flowing by on his bicycle. He was in his sixties and appeared to be doing laps, riding up to the end of the street where it turned into sloppy dirt road, turning around, then heading back past the window. He dawdled along, the slow arc of the pedal moving him forward. His jeans were frayed at the bottoms and spotted with old paint, and his big green gloves rested awkwardly on the handlebars of his girlish bike. It was too small and painted mauve. After a while Helen couldn't help watching when he passed, would lift her tea and sip, follow him the length of the pane. Then she would wait, looking out the side window at the pale green clapboard house, the stretch of ground leading up to it, sparse with trees and covered in rotted leaves. She was pretty sure the house was his, and had noticed many times the name on the mailbox by the road: *Glasskatt*. He would pass again, and she would anticipate how long before his next appearance. The book lay open in her lap. After a while it was like carrying on a conversation.

Then there were sirens, the sound of firetrucks racing along the main road. He pedalled past the window right on time and the sirens got closer. A minute later the sirens had disappeared, had fled right past, but he failed to ride by the window. Helen looked at the clock. She looked out at the empty road.

After a few minutes she gave up on him and turned back to her book, but found that she had lost her place. Must have followed the sirens, she thought, and felt that she had been stood up.

She saw him go past the window a few days later, on foot this time and pushing a baby carriage. He was wearing the same cap, and the same gloves gripped the bar of the carriage. She wandered outside and sat on the step, waiting for him to pass again.

He approached her in time with the train.

"There goes the Triton and Tex," he said, gazing at the train and nodding his head in response to his own statement. "It takes a little of me with it every time it passes." He watched it rattle past, car by car along the tracks. Helen noted that there was no baby in the carriage.

"Oh, just practicing," he said, but he sounded noncommittal. Then he added, "I'm taking up babysitting." His eyes were on the train. He scratched the side of his nose with a big gloved fist, then as an afterthought said, "I'm Al. Live just up the road there." Helen smiled at him briefly then returned to the names on the sides of the boxcars. *Triton* went past on a dozen or so cars, interspersed with cars marked *Tex*. Two others said *Eco Mines*. "It gives you something then takes it away," Al said, meaning the train. Helen listened to him speak against the clang and squeal of the wheels. Then he smiled and waved his hand in front of him as though to dismiss the entire conversation.

There was never really a silence at night. Even with Artie away ("Too drunk," he'd said, "staying over," then hung up) the house made night noises of its own. The wall opposite would creak, a moment later a different one. The hot water heater would start up then die away after a few minutes, the electric heaters click click clicked, keeping the temperature even. Even the refrigerator was audible from the bed. Helen kept the lights off and listened.

Cars fled down the highway at 2:14 in the morning. The sound of them approaching, passing, then disappearing, covered the distance of road and trees. A rise and fall of sound. Helen hadn't noticed before. But she had hoisted the window wide open so that the cool April air would spill across her arms, her neck, her face, like hands brushing against her. She thought of driving into Montreal, right then, of spending the last few hours of the night wandering along empty streets lit up with the feel of temporary abandonment, of a pause sustained. She loved the middle of the night in the city. But Artie had the car, and she was stuck, stuck alone out in the countryside. Her breathing steadied. She fell asleep to the sound of a car passing on the highway, the sound of tires on asphalt and the displacement of air by two thousand pounds and a person she would never meet.

There were things that Helen brought with her from the city that had been impossible to leave behind. She couldn't shake the tiny plot gardens from her mind: ground-floor apartment dwellers had turned and raked the few feet of earth available and filled them with flowers and vegetable greens. At first she thought that the countryside dwarfed the cramped beauty of the city, but slowly this sense had started to reverse itself, until she sat staring out at the glib trees and found herself thinking hungrily of her old street overflowing with considered blooms.

Another thing she hauled out to the countryside with her like cheap luggage was a peculiar vision of Artie as the final test of her ability to share with another her space, her particular take on the world, her pleasure and bitter cynicism. The final attempt. Her patience had worn thin.

That's how she had felt in the first euphoric months of their relationship, had felt pretty sure that it was possible with Artie. And although she had slowly begun to consider this view suspect over the following year and a half, she clung to it just the same, it was easier that way.

Helen never bothered making the bed; Artie didn't, so why should she. But somewhere along the way he had started to reproach her for things like this. It was a silent reproach, a look, or a frown; a circuitous path around the symptoms of his contempt. "Hypocrite," Helen said whenever she caught him at it, but he feigned confusion, said he'd been misunderstood. They were locked to each other by the silence of the woods.

Helen started wondering, grew impatient. She was curious to know how Al spent his days.

"He's probably just a senile old guy," Artie said over dinner. He spoke distractedly.

"I don't think so. But he's got motives." Helen wished she hadn't brought it up. Artie took everything as an argument these days.

"Motives?" Artie said this with exaggerated emphasis, and his eyebrows pinched together mockingly. He rolled green-pea pebbles into a cliff of mashed potatoes with his fork.

"Never mind," Helen said. The house felt too small. She got up from the table giddy and panicked and wanting to get away from Artie. The stairs passed under her feet two at a time. Her heart was racing. She didn't quite mean 'motives', but the word acted as shorthand in her head for the machinations of a mind. She meant that there was a thing that he was working at, whereas she and Artie were working at nothing. She locked the door of the bathroom behind her.

Sleep had not come. It wasn't Artie's snoring that kept her awake, even though she had been able to hear it from time to time through the wall during the night. He had taken to falling asleep on the couch over the past few weeks, and when his back would no longer put up with that, he took to the spare room. When he slept in the spare room he was always careful to let Helen go to bed first.

Helen had been unable to sleep because every time she began to doze off, when she felt the relaxing of muscles and the tension lifting off her, she would get the distinct feeling that Artie was standing above her, talking gently, though she couldn't make out the words, and pulling the blankets around her tighter and tighter until she felt that she would suffocate. And then the quiet image would come to her, clear as day, of the yellow handle end of the axe tilting lightly into the wall, leaning by the back door, and she would sit up wide awake with her heart racing.

The night took forever to end. She only left

the bed when the sky reversed itself, went from black to midnight blue to sapphire, then the light seeped into it full and the sun began to rise. She sat at the kitchen table and stared at the floor, waiting for the kettle to boil. She wasn't thinking about anything now. She gazed down at the linoleum and saw the air waver above it like a mirage, like heat rising.

The window ledge was flaking and bits of old paint stuck to Helen's arms. She peered through the window, just to see what it was like inside the clapboard house. Al Glasskatt was out again with the baby carriage, and Helen had concluded that he lived alone. The living room was immaculate, with the cushions just so and a newspaper carefully refolded at the edge of the coffee table. She spotted a rocking chair pushed up against the far wall. Her rocking chair. She left the window and walked back across the grass.

Making her way through the spring stench of wet rotting leaves and earth, Helen noted how things emerged, settled into relief, then wore away until they disappeared altogether. Millions of years, or a single season. She had found the rocking chair abandoned in an alley in Mile End the spring before, when she and Artie had just begun talking about moving out to the country and renting a house.

"Why, I found it in the garbage," Al said

standing in his doorway, "up there by the main road." He smiled at her sympathetically and pointed up the only road. They both followed the invisible line leading away from his finger. Helen thought, Here is my tiny spot on the planet, and I'm sharing it with this stranger who has stolen my rocking chair out of the garbage. A minute passed while they both looked out at the road, then Al stepped aside and opened the door wider.

"Come on," he said and tugged gently at her arm until she stepped into his house.

Once she was inside Al's house Helen stopped caring about the chair. He gave her tea and put on opera. "You'll like this," he said, and when she looked at him leaning over the record player he was smiling.

"Can you *steal* something out of the garbage?" Artie said. He was leaning over the sink eating a sandwich. "I mean it's in the garbage, it's been discarded. You've given up ownership. Right?" A piece of tomato fell to the floor as he turned to address Helen. His questions were clearly rhetorical.

"That's my chair, Artie, and I didn't give up ownership of it just because someone else tossed it in the garbage. It was stolen." She was sitting on the kitchen table, absently playing with a spoon. She looked down at herself distorted in the spoon, then at the mess of tomato and mayonnaise on the floor. The spoon slipped through her fingers and clanged against the linoleum.

"In principle," Artie said, shoving the last of his sandwich into his mouth. "How's anyone supposed to know it was stolen? You've garbage-picked hundreds of times." He was right, she had dug gleefully through other people's trash many times.

"That's not the point," she said, retrieving the spoon. But there was no resolve in her voice.

Since the weather had turned nice, the days warm and bright and the nights cool and damp, Helen had taken to sitting out on the porch after dark. She was listening, trying very hard to hear. The high cry of the frogs, calling out for mates when the air began to cool, made it difficult for her to be sure of what she was listening for. So she sat for long spells, breathing in wet cedar and pine and listening to the thrum of frogs, singling out one here and there from the others and gauging its distance. When she singled them out, she inevitably had a moment of confusion, and the sound became an amplified crying out of young birds. There would be a slight seizing of her stomach, as though she had walked straight into the blunt end of the banister, and she would feel the backs of her eyes begin to throb. But then she would remember that it was frogs, only frogs. So loud, she thought looking out into the dark. Yet she found it soothing.

Once while she sat out on the porch she heard the click of the door, the rasp across the mat. Artie stood still for a moment, listening. "So loud," he said from behind her. She nodded, without turning around. "Coming in soon?" he asked, his voice quiet against all the calling and answering, and she nodded again, and again her stomach seized slightly, a pain right at the centre. She rose slowly from the chair, and that night she slept with Artie again.

After that she found herself listening for the click of the door, but it didn't come, there was only that once. After a while she stopped sitting out on the porch after dark.

Al had sat her down and suggested tea. He had made her choose: regular or herbal. She thought herbal would be nice. Mint, chamomile, fennel. Or senna leaves. But that's a laxative, he'd said and laughed, we won't give you that. Helen couldn't remember what she had chosen. She vaguely suspected that she had not chosen at all. The house was so tidy, everything folded and placed, edges straight and corners perfectly square. His mother had made the pillows, needlepoint orchids that looked like wasps poised to sting. The pictures on the walls were painted by him. She couldn't decide whether they were good or bad. They were swamped in red she remembered, but thinking about it now, she couldn't recall what they were of.

There were things she remembered, new images in her mind, that came out of that afternoon at Al's. When she tried to think of them, they would not come. She could only remember that there were things he had told her that she hadn't known before. But they came in flashes, jumped out at her when she wasn't looking for them. While she watered her African violets she found herself thinking about the soapstone that could easily be found in deposits all through the mountain, and how it didn't occur naturally in the geological landscape of the area but had been carried down by glaciers long ago. She had never thought of stone as being anything other than permanent, the most solid of things. She had been wrong, it seemed. While she pinched the dead flowers off the plants she saw the room again, saw the bottom of his stairs curving out of sight around the corner and the empty hurricane lamps sitting at either end of the mantle like blind sentries. You have no children, Al had said from the kitchen, and she had been leaning against one of the orchid cushions that kept flipping back and forth between orchid and wasp. She remembered feeling uncomfortable just then. But then he came back in smiling, with a flowery china cup in each hand, each delicate and steaming, and said, Me neither.

What happens when you stop liking the look of your lover? Artie's face had grown sallow, perhaps it had always been, but Helen couldn't take her eyes off the shadows and hollows of his cheeks, the bluntness of his undiscriminating nose. All of his features were suddenly too prominent, bigger than she could take, a familiar image in a warped mirror.

She took to hunting after Artie left for work in the mornings, a timid search through other people's solitude. She looked in windows, trying to be discreet; she told herself she was searching for her things and was not interested in the people who inhabited the houses. People were asleep on their couches in the middle of the day, or sitting up and staring out at nothing. She'd had no idea.

"A lot of people live alone around here," Al said when she told him what she had seen, "most are older, don't know what to do with themselves." Helen detected a bitterness in his voice. "What a thing to do to yourself." He turned to his large bookshelf to continue the search she had interrupted, and Helen thought, Yes, what a thing.

She didn't really care about the furniture. With Artie, though, she felt she had to keep up appearances. He was always talking about consistency. Though it wasn't entirely an act; the furniture seemed to matter more in his company.

He spent most of his evenings over at Tom

and Katia's these days, watching television or playing bridge.

"Who's the fourth?" Helen asked.

"What?" Artie said with his mouth full of toothpaste. Helen watched him fiddle with the taps, toothpaste frothing down his chin while he tried to get the temperature just right. He spat in the sink. "Just some friend of Tom's," he said and put his mouth up to the tap to rinse. Helen thought he responded to her question as though it were an attack. She wrapped her arms around him from behind, she hadn't meant it that way. "He's fucking awful," Artie said more boldly, leaning forward to spit. But then he paused. "Do you mind? I can't move." He looked at her in the mirror, his toothbrush poised above the sink. Helen removed her arms from his waist and left the room.

How do people manage, Helen wondered while she swept the broken glass up off the kitchen floor. The glass of water had slipped from her hand for no reason at all. She felt dazed, realized she was far too tired, out of all proportion with her level of activity. She had taken to doing nothing. Some people can live their lives, she thought, and other people can't. She hadn't managed to get her work done, had had to call up her clients and tell them about the robbery. She thought she had made it sound worse than it was. There's nothing wrong, she thought. Just a little tired. But she had taken on no new projects. Her days slipped past her, disappeared like highway under a car speeding into the night.

Helen dropped in on Al, asked him how the babysitting was going, even though she didn't believe in it. The carriage, she had noticed, was often filled with rocks collected off the mountain. She hoped he would invite her in again for tea, play music and tell her with enthusiasm to listen, just listen, as he had done before, but she caught him on his way out.

"Did I tell you that? I don't think I told you that." He was standing on his front porch, not looking at Helen but pulling things out of his pockets, turning crumpled pieces of paper over in vague examination then returning them to a different pocket. She told him what he had said.

"Oh no no," he said, "I told you the wrong thing." He continued shuffling things from pocket to pocket. "Rocks," he said and smiled. But then his smile disappeared and he said, "That fellow you live with," and stopped. Helen wondered what exchange they had had, what Artie must have said. She should have asked, but she couldn't. She felt she was expected to know already. "He hasn't much tact, has he," Al said, but Helen just stared and said nothing. She didn't like being held responsible for Artie's behaviour, she knew perfectly well how he could be.

Everything bugged her. The way he held his fork, the sound of him blowing his nose. The obvious energy he gave to slamming the door behind him whenever he entered or left the house. Actions that felt like recriminations, for something she had failed to do.

Artie had refused to buy a new television on the grounds that television stole one's initiative. He was kneeling in front of the bookshelf in the living room when he'd said it, pulling books halfway out then pushing them back, hardly looking at what was written on them yet examining the whole of it as though he had never been that close before. As soon as he'd said it he started to squirm. "You know what I mean." Then he set about shrugging his shoulders in his own defence, as though he were simply repeating something that Helen had said first. Artie never said things like that, he didn't give a damn about initiative, and Helen knew that the source of his discomfort was not having found his own words for it before fumbling it on to Helen.

"Who," Helen asked, "did you pick that up from?" Even before it came out she knew that it was the wrong thing to say. All the wind went out of her. Artie, who read newspapers and magazines and rarely looked between the covers of a book, said nothing. "Artie," Helen began. But there was nothing else to say. She turned and walked out of the house, banging the front door shut behind her.

The drive out to the farm where Helen had spent her childhood summers took her only twenty minutes. She knew it was there, had chosen to move out to the area for that reason, but she hadn't been back to see it since the previous summer, just a few weeks before they had left the city for good. No one had lived there for years and it was beginning to fall apart, but she liked to come and see it every once in a while. There had been a milk cow she and her brothers had named Augusta, and chickens that laid their eggs in the bucket of the rusting tractor behind the small barn; the fort they'd built in the woods; the dinners cooked on a hibachi on the front lawn while their parents sat away from the smoke, drinking manhattans with friends who had come up for the weekend. Visiting the farm gave her a feeling of expansiveness. It gave an immediacy to her past that was rarely there, in the same way that catching the scent of spring lilac made her feel strangely whole, because it took her back to her grandmother's garden. It was like reclaiming a piece of an earlier time, a clipping that she could place on the window sill in a glass jar with water and look at, without feeling the need to hurry.

She parked on the shoulder of the road. What had once been a dirt road leading up to the house had narrowed into an overgrown path. The bullrushes had taken over on either side where it had always been swampy, and stood now brittle and yellow, like petrified wheat. Long, bedraggled grass pointed up the wet path. When Helen reached the crest of the small rise in the road she stopped. The house stood before her, the barn off to the left. Both were weather-worn and sagging. The white pine, that for so many years she had watched grow tall and lush and whose soft, draping needles she had run her fingers through just the year before, had been snapped in two by lightning. The upper half lay sprawled out on the damp ground with the broken trunk caught in the lower branches of the tree. Helen looked at the empty house, the barn, the dying tree. She noted the sunshine pouring down, and the hint of green coming up from the earth all around. Not a single cloud in the sky above.

Helen began to cry. She cried so hard that when she walked toward the toppled tree she stumbled over a rock. She wrapped herself in the tree's branches and stroked the long, soft needles, again and again, pressed her face against the delicate needles.

Helen was sitting out on the porch in the early evening, the telephone resting on her shoulder. Artie's mother was telling her about the state of her house, how the subfloor had rotted through and leaks had led the rain down the kitchen wall; the carpet would have to be pulled back and the floor ripped out from the inside. Helen was picturing the dark kitchen, the hot water tank in the corner streaked with grease that had accumulated over the years. She saw the ugly paintings that hung on the living room walls, the old trophies and dingy paperbacks.

The light suddenly changed. Helen looked up. The sky was turning orange and red, there were thick puffs of white cloud like crumpled paper, like notes to herself unheeded, and a silver flicker moving across the sky. She watched the tiny distant plane glide silently across the clouds, watched the lovely light and smelled the air.

"Artie's not here, I'm afraid," she suddenly said to Artie's mother. And then, "A car's just pulled up, I'll have to talk to you later." She pictured a car as she said it. She hung up. The car disappeared. She looked back up at the sky, at the thin white streamer left by the plane.

She'd had enough of watching trains pass. Artie hadn't been home in three days, hadn't even called, so she left no note, packed a bag and walked up to the road where she put out her thumb and was picked up almost right away. They beat the train, racing over the railroad crossing ahead of it, and sped on toward Montreal in an old convertible with the top down. This made conversation impossible, which was a relief.

"My mother," Al had said two days before, standing at Helen's door. He had pulled in his bottom lip when he spoke.

It took some time to sort out the confusion of names, because when Helen asked the people at the funeral parlour which chapel was reserved for Al's mother's service, everyone told her that she was in the wrong place. She gave the name again, but they continued to shake their heads politely. When she spotted Al across the room speaking with an elderly woman, she pointed him out, but the employees of the funeral parlour only shook their heads a little less politely and said that she was mistaken. So when Al said to Helen, It's sweet of you to have come, she couldn't resist the impropriety of asking him directly who owned the house he was living in. "A fellow named Glasskatt," he said without appearing offended, only slightly disoriented by death. All questions were equal.

People sat hip to hip in the pews. The chapel was full. Helen stood at the back and so had a good view of all the bald spots and elderly redheads with their roots coming in grey. She tried not to listen to the careful way in which the minister spoke the dead woman's name, having only recently learned it and so holding it up like a hollowed-out egg before people who had known it for years.

Then back to the daughter's house, Al's sister, where the dead woman's aging son-in-law was bellowing gently at everyone to get out of the kitchen, get out of the narrow hallway, why do people stand in the most insincere places? Nobody asked him what he meant. But they continued to clog up the hallway, dawdling over goodbyes and making it difficult for anyone trying to slip off unnoticed to the washroom at the other end of the house.

After it was over Helen wandered the city, and that's where she saw him, saw Artie sitting at an outdoor café at an intimate table with a woman she had never seen. The context was so strange, the sight so unfamiliar and the city so new again, that she felt no shock, only relief.

It was already May, a hot afternoon, but still only May. Helen thought how the summers seemed unending and yet somehow did not last very long. There was the muddled sense, as she walked on toward the park, that in the summer months she was really asleep, going through the motions of wakefulness; that it was during the winters that she was actually awake. There was the smell of lilac, and something else whose name she couldn't think of. She passed a small patch of garden where a woman stood against a fence. The woman frowned. She was in a sleeveless shirt with her hair bunched up on top of her head in an elastic band. Her arms were crossed and she was smoking a cigarette. She was looking, alternately, far up the street and through the open doorway of her house. The brightness of the sun, the cars glinting past in a flash of repose, the clicking of bicycles changing gears while two people laughed on the sidewalk up ahead. Vague images, all of them, as though in a dream. The light never seemed to end. On days like this, turning on a lamp in the corner of a room was no more than an exercise, like doing scales on an untuned piano. The colour of the narrow lawns had deepened in only a few days.

In the park, the stone monument was engraved in shadows with the creep of moss at its base. Women wearing hats with the brims flipped up at the front sat with books in their laps, a foot each on the lower rung of a baby stroller. Trucks were assembled at the centre of the pond. A chipped bronze statue of two cherubs swung gently from ropes and a hoist, as though pulled from the flames of a burning church. It was being carefully lowered into place at the centre of the asphalt pond where it would soon spew water from an empty urn. Then there was the creak of plastic wheels as a mother rose, slipped her book amid hot blankets, then veered around the pond and disappeared.

Helen couldn't think; her brain would not go. Back in the city for the first time in nearly a year, and she could not think. The details of the winter would not come back to her. Yet there was a certain seduction to the slow flow of thought, the thick honey flow. She was content just to be in the park in the bright, bright sun. After an hour, though, of watching people move about, arrive in the park and leave, she felt she had fallen behind, as though the city had grown strange in her absence, as though its language had evolved, and she had not kept up.

But then she rose and began to walk, left the park behind her. A firetruck rolled lazily up the street beside her. The young driver, with cropped hair, white T-shirt and firefighter suspenders, rested an elbow out the open window. He watched Helen walking along the street, and when he caught her eye he retrieved the cigarette from behind his ear, slipped it between his lips and smiled. Helen walked on.